Only the Raven Knows

To Barbara,

Enjoy the book —

Robin Wood
2004

"Well, I'm ready. You can belay me down while I rappel with the rope I tied around the big rock"

Sunny looked stupidly at the rope he handed to her.

"I said, belay me down Night."

Sunny jumped. "You stupid ass. I'm so scared I'd probably drop you if I tried to belay right now.

"Oh Night girl, I'm sorry!" Bran put his arms around her. Sunny dropped her head against his chest

"You're going down into that deep dark hole. What if something happened? At this moment I couldn't go in and help you.

"Yes you would. I know you. You would fight the devil if you thought it was the right thing to do. As far as I can see, I'll only be going down about fifteen feet. Since I'm over six feet that leaves only nine feet for me to drop. Now, come on sweetheart and get behind that big rock to belay me down."

Sunny lifted her face to look at him, concern in her eyes. He lowered his head and kissed each eye, then her delectable mouth. Even cussing him out, it's still delectable, he thought.

Only the Raven Knows

A ROMANTIC ADVENTURE NOVEL

To see the ocean from the top of a mountain is the best of both worlds

Robin Wood
2004

Robin Wood

Only the Raven Knows
by Robin Wood
www.xlibris.com/wood.html

I love to hear from any reader:
You can visit us at *r-g-wood@juno.com* or write to the author:
Robin Wood, P.O. Box 1125, Concrete, WA 98237

This book was printed in the United States of America.

To order additional copies of this book, contact:
Xlibris Corporation
1-888-795-4274
www.Xlibris.com
Orders@Xlibris.com
20209

THE BOOK IS DEDICATED TO
THE MANY WONDERFUL PEOPLE WE KNEW WHILE WORKING
FOR THE MOUNT BAKER NATIONAL FOREST
AND THE NORTH CASCADES NATIONAL PARK.

Dear Reader,

I don't think any book could be written without the help of other people. My book started with a dream. My daughter, Diane suggested that I write it down. I did and then the 'What ifs?' started. While we waited for her new house to be finished, we did an outline and I started my new love of writing.

Many people helped when I had questions. The 240 Z car was my son, Rick's. When I needed another fancy car, Toni LeClare at one time had a MG. The weight of a bear came from my hunting family, Randy, Ryan and Ramsey. Naturally it had to be the biggest and best bear they had ever seen. The mini-crew was aptly named and daughter, Wendy worked for the Job Corps at that time. She later was married in the little church. My Park Service husband, Jerry and I hiked the trails and did mileage and observations of terrain. Son, Ross contributed a scene about the gold creek.

I stretched the truth on the crew quarters and created a scene on the West Bank trail that I had to walk out on a bluff to see. After all that I expect to see Bran and Sunny on that trail whenever I hike it. I visited cemeteries to find one that had really old headstones in it. Imagination or not, I say a prayer when I go by the one in Hamilton.

It wasn't easy, but I did go out of my way not to have my characters be any of the wonderful people we lived and worked with at the Marblemount Ranger Station.

Last but not least are the Writer's of the North Cascades: Mardi, Fawn, Heather and Melissa, who critiqued it and my Aunt Louise, friends: Nancy, Judy, Karen and daughter, Diane who helped with correction. All the rest of the mistakes are the computer and mine.

I sincerely hope you enjoy the book as much as I enjoyed writing it.

Robin Wood

COVER STORY

CARVED RAVEN

In 1978 I was into Indian lore. My daughter, Diane was carving totems with a chainsaw. I decided to carve a Raven with a chisel and hammer. Later I burnt it with a blowtorch and then brushed it with a wire brush. My son, Ross thought the Raven would be a good picture for the cover of the book. He took the digital picture and cropped it. Also, I was into Hex signs and meanings so I carved on the back of the Raven, *'River stay away from my door'*. It has since been placed in the yard where it has gathered moss all these many years. And the river stayed away from our door.

Contents

CHAPTER 1

WASHINGTON STATE

Fall of the year 1889

The savory smell of venison stew permeated the air. The young woman looked around the cozy cabin. Everything was in order and freshly cleaned. Rafe would be home sometime today. Oh, how she missed him. Pouring tea into a cup, she took it over to the rocking chair by the window. The advantage of sitting there gave her a clear view of the meadow and a panoramic view of the snow capped mountains of the Upper Skagit Valley. Her thoughts went rambling . . . .

Rafe's only been trapping a week. He'd just gone across the Skagit River to the old gold mines up Ruby creek. That's not all that far. I sure hope the trapping pays off for him. If it was summer and he was working the gold mine, I wouldn't worry so, but this early snow will make him wet and hungry. He was always so happy to return home. This time he'll be concerned for both of us.

A tender smile curved Katy's lips as she looked over at the unique cradle holding their small son. Oh, how proud Rafe was when his son had been born just a short time ago. It had been hot in mid August. She had given birth to the baby right out in their mountain meadow in the shade of her favorite tree. It had been her choice. The tranquility of the meadow dispelled her fears of impending childbirth. Rafe had wanted her to go out of the mountains, but she had begged to stay here at the cabin. She didn't really know the people down in the valley anyway.

In preparation for fatherhood, Rafe had hand-hewed the cradle from cedar. He had pitched and pegged it to put the cradle together. The carvings on it showed the influence of the local Indians. Rafe admired their art and had incorporated the Raven symbol on the hood of the cradle, the carving extending down the sides to end with a knobbed clawed foot. This kept the cradle from rocking too far forward. It had been her idea to have the heart carved on the end panel. Her blue eyes twinkled as her generous lips smiled at the thought.

Dutch people liked hearts and flowers. She remembered how her mother and father had tried so hard to keep a little of their heritage when they'd come to the new country. Even though she could hardly remember the old country, as she had been only ten years of age, she'd wanted to follow that tradition in memory of her folks.

Katy had sewn every little stitch into the baby's layette, including the coat-of-many-colors, which had given the baby his proud name of Joseph. Material was hard to come by, so every little scrap had to be used. The coat had turned out cute she thought.

She and Rafe had done a lot of things in their two years together. In fact, looking around the cabin reminded her that Rafe was a very good craftsman. If he chose, he could make a living in the city with his feel for style and his knowledge of wood. The cabin was built into a cave. Its cedar-pole rafters had been peeled and cured in the cave, as was the rest of the hewn wood.

Hand-split cedar shakes graced the small portion of the cabin that was exposed at the cave's entrance. Thick shutters covering the four windows, were now open. Rafe had hauled glass in over Sourdough Mountain on the back of old Molly, the mule. This had been a tremendous undertaking for him in an area so remote, but so wonderful for light and the view. The door was a thick slab holding out all intruders including the cold. Rafe planned to carve designs in it eventually.

Rafe had lived in the cave during his gold mining adventures. He had ventured up and down the Skagit River, but always came back to the cave. Its lure seemed compulsive. He had made sure no trail led here. During those days you could lose your life for a few ounces of gold and Rafe had done better than most in finding the illusive treasure. He was a good man. He hadn't spent it all on a trip to the big city like so many men did. Instead, he had ordered him a bride! She knew this from the many times he had talked to her about it during the long winter months.

It had been her good fortune to have answered that advertisement. Life had been good back East until that bad winter had come. Hurricanes had taken the lives of so many fishermen. Influenza had taken its toll on those men, women and children who had waited for the fishermen at home. Her folks had died, also. She had survived the flu, but Kurt, her fiancée, had perished. He'd been swept overboard while on the fishing boat.

Life at this point had been very bleak. No family, no fiancée and the only work had been in a sweathouse making clothes. She was a fine seamstress, but work for a young woman was hard to find. She felt lucky to have had any job at all.

Then, one windy day, that newspaper had literally blown into her face. The advertisement said, "*Wanted, 20'ish God-fearing woman able to withstand hardship, loneliness. Must be healthy, strong. No plowing. If compatible! Matrimony. A-2, Seattle.*" Now, where was Seattle?

It had taken about six months to get to Seattle. She'd

brought her unused dowry with her. The set of fine Delft dishes had been her mother's brought over from Holland. Her wedding dress was her own fine handiwork, hoping she might use it if this mountain man did marry her.

'Mountain Man' had reminded her of a hairy smelly bear of a man. It had been a real pleasure to find Rafe clean, with his beard trimmed and a quiet demeanor. He was a bear of a man though, tall and very dark with piercing black eyes. The scar above one eye and a slightly crooked nose, souvenir from a fistfight, showed the Irish in the man.

He had wooed her like an Irishman, in a flamboyant style, but with his quiet way. She had loved him truly. They were married. Their wedding rings were made from the gold nuggets he had panned from Ruby Creek.

She glanced at her ring. What memories those were. He had brought her to the Upper Skagit Valley by ship out of Seattle, sternwheeler up the Skagit, stage coach until the road ran out, then canoe and finally horseback, with walking in rough spots At times she thought she'd die from tiredness. About the time she thought she couldn't make it, a roadhouse would appear as if by magic. A bed, a bath and food would do wonders; Rafe had never taken his husbandly rights on the trip. He had just held and cherished her. His rights had belonged to this cabin, his eagle aerie here in the high mountains. He had crafted his home for a mate like other wild animals; his lair, his den, his aerie.

A gurgling noise brought Katy out of her reverie. Bending over the cradle, she crooned in a hushed voice. "Hey, little fellow, you shouldn't be awake yet. Sleep now so you'll be awake when your daddy gets home." There was a soft burp from this dark haired, dark-eyed, sweet smelling babe. Katy rocked the crib. It rocked up and down like a rocking chair, not sideways like most cradles. Rafe had not paid much attention to cradles and thought that was the way it should rock. No thrashings back and forth, ride it like a horse he had thought. He even had a footrest on the end so a foot tapping, to a strumming guitar, could keep the cradle rocking. It worked very well for both father and son.

All was quiet. Katy set the table with her Delftware and placed candles on each side of the red leaves of the huckleberry brush centerpiece. She had collected them on her way to the outhouse that morning to relieve herself. The frost had really made them beautiful this year. There had even been a few berries left on the branches.

The stew smelled good. She checked the sourdough bread. It was a lovely shade of brown as only a wood stove can do. She took it out of the oven. A quick flip of the pan and the bread fell free to cool on the clean dishtowel. She stoked the wood stove and dampered it down. Katy looked out of the window. It was nearly noon. Rafe should be coming soon. She poured a cup of tea. Salal tea made from the leaves of the salal bush was refreshing. However, she would be glad to go out someday and bring back some good English tea.

It was just after noon. A man with a pack on his back, rifle in one hand and a stringer of fish hanging from a notched stick in his other hand labored up the mountain. From habit, he didn't take any trail. It had been several years since most of the miners had left, but habit for survival was strong. Rafe caught himself hurrying at times. His thoughts raced ahead of him to the cabin. He was finding it harder and harder to leave Katy alone while he ran the trap line. He enjoyed her company.

It would be great when Katy and the babe could go with him again. He had fixed the cradle so it could be strapped on like a backpack, Indian style. Katy could strap it on and carry the babe. Come to think of it, why should she have to carry him? He could! But, then she'd have to carry the camp stuff and traps. He let out a sigh . . . you never win! Wouldn't you know it'd always be called work!

He hiked on up the mountain through the heavily treed hillside. Early snow still lay in open patches. Squirrels were chattering at him while scampering to hide their cones in stashes under fallen logs.

He and Katy had done the trap line last winter. He enjoyed setting up camp and cuddling Katy at night to keep her warm. A grin crossed his face, changing the dour lines in it to a dimple. A few times they'd both been hot enough to melt the snow shelter. Her skin was so soft. God! He'd better keep his mind on the trail. He'd walk off a cliff if he didn't watch out.

Stopping to get his wind, he looked around. Fall was beautiful with all the colors around, though this early snow had nearly knocked all the leaves off the bushes around him. The snow was still heavy higher up on the mountain. The deer were plentiful. He'd take the babe out hunting as soon as he could walk. Next time they went out to the valley, he'd look for a gun for the little fellow. Probably a twenty-two-pump action rifle to start with. You never knew if a kid would be right or left handed until they grew older. A pump action would work for either hand. The bolt action made it harder to use. He could shape the stock to fit either cheek.

Now, that Katy-love, she was a right good shot. He'd taught her to shoot that first year, both for protection and for fun. God! How he loved that girl. What good luck to find the most beautiful girl coming down the gangplank in Seattle that day was his. He hadn't let on to anyone how she had affected him. He supposed she was tall to anyone else, but to his six foot or better, she was just right. And, that shoulder length, golden yellow hair from her Dutch ancestry, well, it just glowed about her.

Lying on their bed with that golden halo around her, she looked like an angel. Those eyes as blue as the lupine growing in the meadow—. Bloody hell! If he didn't get home soon, he'd be breaking the buttons on his buckskin pants. It was rutting season all right.

Sipping her tea, Katy looked out the window for the hundredth time she thought. The sun was still on the meadow, their meadow. Rafe so carefully pulled up the small trees growing there. A tree pulled up now was one less stump to pull out later, he'd always told her. The grazing deer kept the rest of it pruned back. Even mountain goats came by in the winter. They had a small garden, but the high fence necessary to keep the deer out, also kept a lot of sun out. It didn't do all that well. Most of the vegetables they needed came from the McMillan Ranch, up Big Beaver about five miles away, or down in the valley, a hazardous journey over Sourdough Mountain. It took old 'muley' Molly a day to traverse around Sourdough Mountain just to bring supplies from down there. Katy was sure Molly hated her, upstaging the mule's place in Rafe's affection.

Old Molly was their lifeline to the outside. Rafe had told her the Gorge was impassible with the raft. He didn't know anyone who had tried it and made it. But then, a person never went out often enough to hear if anyone did make it. They usually just went out and never came back.

Katy had seen the Gorge. It was a spectacular cascade of boiling water. Just above the Gorge the river flattened out enough to get the raft across with old Molly aboard. Rafe also had a birch bark canoe. Katy didn't like the canoe. The river looked too wild for a canoe, but Rafe had no trouble with it. It seemed to be only a few strokes for him to get across the river. This entire crossing was necessary to get to the mining claim in summer and that part of his trap line in winter.

A movement to the left of the meadow caught Katy's eye. Could that be Rafe? She could never guess where he'd appear because he never took the same trail. No, that must have been something else. Just then, down at the bottom of the meadow, a big man with a maroon and green knit hat stepped out of the shadows of the timber. Rafe! Katy grabbed her hand knit shawl of the same material as Rafe's hat from the peg beside the great cedar door. A quick glance at the babe showed he was still asleep. She burst out into the bright afternoon sun at a dead run headed for the big man, her hair streaming out behind her, excitement evident in all her movements.

Rafe glanced towards the cabin. Ah! There was his Katy-love running towards him, that stream of gold hair flying behind her. He started to run in a lope, as only a man burdened by his pack can do, his arms swinging wide, a stringer of fish dangling from the left and rifle in the right.

Suddenly, from the edge of the meadow between Rafe and Katy, a black shape charged. The she-bear's great cry of rage halted the two people. Her rumbling attack was directed towards the larger of the two objects in her way. He had that pointed object that had hurt her. She knew her cubs were just across the meadow eating grubs batted out of a rotting stump. Her bloody side ached from the encounter with these same types of creatures on the other side of the mountain. Her only thought was to kill these creatures that might harm her cubs like they had hurt her.

In the seconds it took to register in Rafe's mind, this bear was mad and looked like it was charging Katy, he yelled.

"Run! Katy-love run!"

Katy stopped. Seeing the bear immobilized her with fear. About then, two more bears broke out from the other side of the meadow. This was too much for Katy, she turned and ran.

"The rifle! The rifle, Rafe!" Her haunting cries echoed through the high mountain meadow.

Rafe had his hands full, with the stringer of fish in one hand and the rifle in the other. His mind went into action. Get rid of the fish; the bear might stop to eat them. He heaved them as hard as he could at the bear. He saw two more bears coming out into the meadow. Cubs! No wonder the she-bear was mad. He saw Katy take off towards the cabin. The fish didn't stop the bear. He dropped his pack as it slipped and hindered his use of the rifle. He didn't really want to kill the mother bear. She's so close now! He fired as she charged. Her full five hundred pounds thrust into him. The gun went flying. Rafe could feel the bear biting into his shoulder. The blows with his fist just sunk into the hair and winter fat of the she-bear.

Katy reached the cabin. Her rifle was ready by the door. She grabbed it up and rushed back out to help Rafe. Subconsciously, she closed the door to protect the baby. The cubs were eating on the fish. No threat! But! Oh God! The huge bear was mauling Rafe. Katy kept running. The cubs were startled and shied away, but went back eating on the fish. Katy was about twenty-five feet away now. She stopped to get a shot off. She screamed at the bear to stop. The bear didn't hear her, but raised its head to get a better hold on its hated object.

Katy shot. By the grace of God she hit the bear. The bear was dead even as it gained another bite, giving a couple of shakes before it collapsed, rolling off the man, but taking most of his shoulder in her unforgiving jaws. With no thought to her own safety, Katy rushed to help Rafe. Rafe, just barley alive, moaned.

"Katy-love. Katy-love." The words were so faint, but filled with great fear for Katy.

"Rafe, my love! Oh God! Are you alive? Oh Rafe!" She was kissing his face, tears streaming down her face. His blood was all over. It had to be stopped. She ripped her petticoat loose making pads to press into the holes, then strips to tie them in place.

"Oh Rafe! Don't die! Come back to me." She kept talking to him as she nursed the many wounds. Both shoulders were nearly gone, but Katy didn't register the damage in her ministrations. Rafe groaned. He was still alive! She must get him to the cabin.

"Rafe! Wake up! You've got to walk," she moaned. She didn't realize the blood on his pants had come from his thigh. However, as in some cases, Rafe woke up. He felt very little pain. The ringing in his ears was about all that registered. He made it to his feet mainly because Katy was literally pulling him up, her strong frame a plus at this moment. They lurched past the cubs, who just stared uneasily at the creatures.

Katy made it to the cabin. It was a real trick to get the door open and hold Rafe, but somehow she did it. She started for the bed. Rafe stumbled. His super-human shot of adrenaline had just run out. She couldn't hold him. In slow-motion Rafe collapsed to their floor. He was shaking from shock. Katy ran to the bed, grabbed the quilt folded on the end of it, and brought it back to put gently over and around Rafe.

She noticed the fresh blood on his pants. In a trance, she found some clean dishtowels and her scissors. She cut the buckskin pants up the leg to the injured area. The pants were very slippery, as leather gets when it's wet. She bandaged the leg. It was turning blue from bruising. She propped his leg up with a chunk of firewood hoping to stop the blood. This was a stroke of luck she thought as it did stop the flow of blood that was seeping from the wounds. Rafe quit shaking. He fell into a deep sleep.

The baby started to fuss. Like a zombie, Katy went to the baby, picked him up, changed his wet nappy and the started to nurse him. She slowly rocked back and forth on the bed, as much to comfort herself, as to comfort the baby.

Being an inexperienced Easterner had not prepared her for this kind of emergency.

"Oh Rafe! I need you," wailed the frightened woman.

Katy tried to think what to do. Old Molly had been turned loose for the winter to forage wherever she could. Only Rafe would know how to get her. That's out! But Katy knew Rafe needed medical help.

The McMillan's Ranch was about five miles away, but to go there was even farther from medical help. No! Remember that leg. Katy wondered how Rafe made it to the cabin. She only knew that fright had given her super-human strength to help him.

The river! If she could get Rafe to the raft, maybe she could pole it down to civilization. The baby squirmed. She put him over her shoulder and patted his bottom gently.

She remembered Rafe had said no one had ever made it through the Gorge. He also said he'd never heard of anyone making it because he didn't get outside to find out. Maybe, just maybe she could do it. Her mind raced.

She'd need something to drag him on. The quilt? Her eyes were on the bearskin rug on the floor by the bed, but not seeing it. Suddenly they did focus. His deerskin pants were slippery. The bearskin rug would pull easily after it got wet. In fact, the hair side would slide even better with the help of the snow and not have to be wet.

A small burp from the baby brought her back to the present. Their little Joseph must be the best baby in the whole world. He was asleep again. For a moment her heart swelled with pride. Katy put him in his cradle. Of course! The straps to the cradle! She could strap the babe to her back.

She looked out the window. The bear cubs were by their dead mother. There was about four hours of daylight. Would that be enough time? No time to lose. She dragged the bearskin rug over by Rafe. She flipped it over pulling the hair side next to the floor. Now, she needed some rope to help tie Rafe on, and to tie the legs of the bear hide to shape a harness. There was rope in the storeroom farther back in the cave.

Taking her cup of tea with her to the cave, she drank it as she got the rope. Leaving the cup and saucer there with only one thing on her mind, she rushed back into the cabin slamming the door shut. Next, clean nappies for the babe. Pack light! She rushed around. She would need strength. Seeing the cooling bread on the counter, she ripped off a piece and ate it as she finished her collection. She tied everything in an old, gray wool blanket left over from Rafe's mining days.

She fitted the straps to the cradle. Next came the rabbit skin bunting she had made from the skins Rafe tanned. It would keep the babe warm. She would put that on him after she got Rafe out the door. She went over to Rafe and tried to roll him onto the bearskin. My God, he was heavy. She stood over him and pulled harder. Rafe let out a groan of agony.

"Katy-love! The bear! Run, run, run." Rafe passed out on the last murmur.

"Rafe my love," she talked to him. "I can't stand to hurt you but I've got to."

She finally rolled him onto the bearskin rug, and tied him inside. He was very white but still breathing. She crawled between the tied bear legs and pulled. After a tug it moved very well. She opened the door and pulled him outside. Rafe groaned several times.

Going back inside for the babe, she put him into his bunting. Her diary waited on the bedside table, left out when she had been writing this morning. Quill and ink ready, habit made her quickly scribble into it. *"Rafe hurt by bear attack. Taking raft. Rafe needs medical care. Taking Joseph in his cradle and Rafe on a bearskin stretcher."* Blotting the ink, she carefully put the diary back into the drawer of the beautifully crafted cedar bedside table.

Reaching down, she picked up the cradle and quickly strapped the baby into it papoose style. He let out a soft sigh. Sliding her arms into the straps on the cradle, one band over her forehead, she was ready to go. Her hips fit snuggly between the rockers. The blanket with the supplies in it was in her hand. Her eyes did a quick study of the cabin. Her beautiful home was a mess, food on the stove, blood on the floor, the soiled blanket left where it fell. No time to clean, Rafe needed help now.

Going out the door, she closed it tightly. Oh—the shutters! Better close those over the windows to keep the animals out. Then after climbing into the homemade harness, she started down the mountain to find the raft, pulling Rafe in the bearskin, with the baby on her back and the sack of supplies in her hand.

Two ravens circled the meadow, ever watchful, circling higher and higher, silhouetted against the clear blue sky. Their cawing grew fainter. Katy looked up once but continued on her urgent quest.

CHAPTER 2

THE GORGE

I t had been a long down hill haul. Rafe had cried out in agony several times, spurring Katy on when she would have rather stopped. She was exhausted. The raft was anchored out of the main stream, protected by a huge boulder. The water was running very high, probably due to the early snow and heavy rains. She put the cradle down. The baby started to cry, but Katy didn't have time to attend to him right now. She hauled on the lines to the raft. She had to get it as near to the bank as possible. The ties were tight but Rafe had showed her how to loosen his special knots. She pulled the raft up close. It was still a drop down to the raft. She would really kill Rafe pulling him on to that. There were quite a few poles lying around. Katy took them to form a bridge from shore to the heavy cedar logs of the raft.

The babe was screaming. She untied him from his cradle to nurse him. Sitting beside Rafe, she gently stroked his forehead, talking to him and the babe. She was so afraid. The

tears came again. No time for tears! She burped the babe and
tied him in his cradle again.

She took the cradle out onto the raft and placed it there
before she went back for Rafe. Dragging him over the poles,
quickly pulling him as the poles began to separate, she made
it. He was on! The raft rocked, splashing water over the up-
river edge. Positioning him closer to the middle where there
was a hitching rail for old Molly, she secured him and the cradle.
She grabbed the smallest of the poles, laying it beside the cradle
to brace both it and Rafe. A couple more sticks from shore
placed under the rockers kept the cradle from rocking.

Now, she untied the lines. Although the river was very high,
and boiling out passed the huge rock, the backwater was
reasonably calm. She poled towards the main stream.

"Here goes nothing. It's do or die!" she cried.

The roar of the canyon was ahead. The water grabbed them
like an angry force. No more poling. Even if she had known
how to steer this bucking monster, she couldn't have, her fears
were so great she was trembling. She collapsed next to Rafe's
head with one arm on the cradle, the other hugging Rafe.
She prayed.

They shot like a bullet through the rapids. The mighty cedar
logs of the raft bounced off the sheer walls of the Gorge, the
Devil's Elbow and Devil's Stepping Stones, were quickly
traversed over and around. Katy knew the names depicted a
dangerous corner of the Gorge with rocks sticking out of the
water like stepping stones of a giant. The high water had
covered them, but the elbow was still there.

Possibly this was a first in history, if anyone were to know, an
impossible journey on a raft had passed though the mighty
gorge into calmer waters were Katy's thoughts as she finally
looked up, but not dropping her inertia of fear yet.

She noticed signs of civilization. A fence ended at the river.
There was a huge clearing, with stumps sticking out of the
snowy ground. She thought this might have been a miner's
camp leftover from the mining days. It looked different from

the river. Or; she could be as far down as Goodell's Portage. She jumped up and started to shout.

The roar from the canyon was still loud. She grabbed the pole lashed to the raft, normally used to steer it. It was broken off below the water. She reached for the shorter pole that, by now, was wedged under Rafe. He groaned. She tried that pole. It was too short. They drifted farther down stream. Katy had no idea how far they might drift, but at least they were headed towards medical help. She sat down again cradling Rafe's head, one hand on Joseph's cradle. She had got them this far, but how to get them to civilization and shore was another story.

The raft bumped and careened quickly down the swift, rain-swollen river and at times through more canyons. They floated for what seemed like hours. The red alpenglow was in the sky turning the river a purplish red and the mountains to frozen pink strawberry dessert. She spotted another raft tied to the bank, but no one was around. It wouldn't be long now until it got dark. Katy hoped someone would see them. She was cold and wet.

Rafe had opened his eyes once and looked at her and said "Katy-love," before passing out again. The babe was actually sleeping. The river rocked him to sleep and the rabbit skin bunting had kept him drier than they were.

Katy wasn't looking. The raft was coming up on another narrow spot in the river. Farther below them, a jagged rock stuck up out of the middle of the river like a misplaced pyramid. The current grabbed the raft. They picked up speed in the narrow channel. With a tremendous impact the swift moving raft hit the rock, slid up the side and was launched into space like an arrow. It did a slow motion rolling flip. On the first impact, the cradle slipped backwards and lightly spun off into the water. It rode the surging current like a tiny catamaran. Katy screamed, "Joseph!" and grabbed for the cradle just as she was thrown into the air.

She and Rafe landed in the water close together. Katy grabbed for him wrapping her hands in the ropes entwined with the bearskin, her eyes searching for Joseph as she clung to Rafe in the raging water, her frantic screams unheard in the roar of the river. The couple floated in the icy cold water until both were pulled under, feeling nothing due to exposure to the elements. A head bobbed once or twice to the surface, and then all was quiet. The mighty Skagit River accepted its sacrifices as it had many times before. A small piece of debris followed the overturned raft, bobbing gently along, hugging the shoreline, unaware of the tragedy that had just occurred.

Not too far down the stream from where the accident happened, the local Indians had set their nets. The Coho salmon were having a good run. The high water had been a big help. It was getting dark. Something was sure bothering the ravens thought Eli Swift River as he pulled his nets, slowly, removing the fish as he did so. The ravens were flying from tree to tree, cawing loudly.

Ignoring the ravens, he kept pulling the net in. His nets had worked out very well. The fish would feed his growing family. His mate had given birth to a male baby this past summer. Male children were a joy to the tribe. Although, he realized a female child would be worth her weight in skins when she took a man.

His good mate was quite a woman. She had woven this fish net from cedar strips, her long black hair, and nettles soaked and stripped into strings. The nettles were tricky to pick. They stung with their hair-like barbs. She loved to weave. His hat was horsehair, bird feathers, and anything else she could get her hands on. He'd had a few fights over this hat. Everyone wanted it; or one like it. His kids were well clothed because of her. In perverse thinking, he fed them well. He was a native hunter and fisherman.

Eli's black eyes scanned the river. He had better get the nets out. All that floating debris would tear them apart. There was just enough light to remove the rest of the fish. He pulled his last net. His eyes were on the first of the fish as a large piece of debris went by. A closer inspection might have recognized parts of a raft. Eli gave another pull. He looked up as something hit the exposed part of the net closest to him. Now what on earth was that? He pulled a little harder. Almost losing the object, he flipped the net to reinforce the hold and pulled again. A shocked Eli reached down and lifted up a water soaked cradle.

His Indian Mission schooling, nearly forgotten, came to mind. "Holy Moses!" he exclaimed, fish forgotten, as he headed for his homestead, a stalwart young Indian in a hurry with his arms full of cradle and a soaking wet, whimpering baby.

CHAPTER 3

THE RANGER STATION

One hundred years later:
1989 WASHINGTON STATE CENTENNIAL YEAR

The little red Volkswagen car bounced jauntily up Highway 20. It seemed to be as happy to escape the confines of the city as its driver. Summer vacation! What a wonderful word. An escape for three months of the year! Sunny had been asked to teach a summer class, but luckily her job had come through to work as a Park Ranger for the summer in the North Cascades National Park.

To Sunny, it was the next best thing to living in the mountains forever. It wasn't that she didn't like her teaching job. She did. But, after three years of working as a summer Park Ranger, she wished she had gone back to college and changed her major to Forestry. This was the life she loved. Remote, where the air was pure and life was lived at a slower pace.

This summer was exciting because she'd never worked west

of the Cascades before. Stehikin was in Eastern Washington. She loved it there too, but now she was about to experience a summer on Ross Lake in the North Cascades National Park. She had spent three summers listening to short wave radio talks between the two areas. Sunny's thoughts were stilled as she came to a straight stretch in the road. Ahead the mountains rose to white capped peaks. To her right the Skagit River majestically flowed towards the ocean about sixty miles away. A side turnout showed a small rest area. Almost on its own, the Volkswagen swung over to stop at the rest area.

She jumped out. Wow! You could smell the mountains. The soft breeze flowing through the huge maple trees along the bank of the river gave off a sweet scent. The church across the field near the base of a mountain must have a beautiful view through its arched windows. She wasn't sure, but she thought she wasn't far from Marblemount. Marblemount Ranger Station would be her headquarters for the summer.

Sunny got back into the car. She had to get checked in. A few more miles and sure enough, she broke over the timbered rise and there was a wide valley, completely surrounded by mountains. A few more bends in the road brought her to the side road that led to the station.

At the end of the road near the base of a mountain, was a cozy cluster of buildings. She knew this was home and office to a bunch of people who looked after the many areas of the North Cascades National Park and Recreation area. It was a well-known fact that you either loved the park or hated it, depending on your own personal views and livelihood.

The loggers usually hated to see the trees locked up without being put to good use. If you were a hunter, the game was always better on the other side of the imaginary fence. Those who worked for the Park usually loved it and Sunny worked for the Park, so sight unseen, she loved it. Now, seeing the office area nestled in its backdrop of trees, she appreciated the quaint looks of it, and this wasn't even the real part of the

Park she would be working in. That was still farther up the highway and into the heart of the mountains.

Sunny parked in front of the office complex. Inside, the office was a hum of activity. People were asking about hiking. New employees were being checked in. Personnel in different offices were all busy and the static of the short wave radio crackled its importance in the scheme of things. It seemed everyone worked on Sunday, which was true, as Sunny knew.

Two uniformed women were doing most of the checking in of new employees. Sunny was escorted over to a desk area and treated to a lovely smile from one of the ladies. After a quick check-in, she was shown to the bunkhouse just across the way and told to pick a bunk.

Thanking the office personnel and knowing she would get to know these people later, Sunny went in the bunkhouse to look her new home over. It was strangely quiet, but sure to be humming soon. Sunny strolled back outside and around the office complex to bring her car to the parking area closer to the bunkhouse.

A few bunks were taken and she hoped she inadvertently didn't stick her stuff in with a gentleman. She knew all the places were co-ed now but you usually had your own gender if you had to share a room. More than two in a room, you took your chances and were happy to even get a bed. Going back outside by way of the back door, she sat down on the steps. A stand of Red Oak trees, not native to this area, graced the back lot growing next to the hillside. Cow Heaven Mountain started in gently rolls here before reaching its mile high status.

To her right she noticed a very expensive looking motor home pulled back into the trees. A beautiful black sports car was parked in front of it. Sunny idly wondered who could afford that kind of lifestyle on Park Ranger wages. Maybe it was a VIP coming to work in one of the campgrounds. VIP meant Volunteer in the Park. This worked very well for retired, active people wanting to be out in the mountains.

She decided to go for a walk around the well cared for

compound. It was getting on toward five in the evening, and everyone would be going home for the night. Tomorrow, starting at eight in the morning would be the big day for all the new personnel. It would take a week of orientation and training to get on the schedule everyone would work. She wondered which days she would get off. It didn't matter to her anyway.

At eight sharp the next morning she quietly took a seat to listen to the Park Naturalist's discourse on Park expectations. She touched her tongue to her upper lip and slowly slipped it across sensually. She didn't think about the action, as a cold sore seemed to be forming there. Her mind was in the area of listening to the tall, dark and handsome ranger.

The ranger getting ready for his talk to the new group of summer personnel, let his eyes wander over the group. This is what you did when you were talking, never really settling on anyone person, just focusing on someone to make a point. You still just treated them as a sea of faces, especially when you gave this same speech time after time.

"Good morning ladies and gentlemen. I'm Bran Donovan. I'm a mining engineer on special assignment to catalog mines in this area. I'm speaking to you in lieu of the regular Park Naturalist who is at a six weeks training school at Harpers Ferry, West Virginia. While I'm here; and also after the regular Park Naturalist returns, I plan to finish studying the mining that went on in the Upper Skagit Valley in the late eighteen hundreds. I'll be visiting as many sites as I can find. Sometimes I'll ask one or more of you to go along. This will be with the permission of your boss. Before long I'll know who will be of the most help on this project. I'll be checking your applications for studies or hobbies relating to my project."

He paused before continuing, "This is a very interesting geographical and historical area you've chosen to work in this summer. It's not only beautiful, with its rugged mountains and

pure streams, but full of history, even if it's considered recent
to most of U.S. of A."

Bran stopped long enough to look the group over. This
usually made a point in the audience's mind. "The Gold Rush
in 1858 opened up the country but was spasmodic both in the
Skagit and Cascade drainage's. Many claims changed from gold
to copper with talc mining continuing up to the present. Talc
is only being used for carvings right now. There has been a lot
of history lost behind the hydroelectric dams, but the dams
are certainly history unto themselves."

Bran looked around again. "I'll also be working with Tyson
Tubbs, our Chief of Indian Affairs," A laugh from the group
broke Bran's concentration.

"Pardon the pun!" A grin slashed his austere features. "I
have many Indian relatives living in Skagit County. Although
I've never lived here, we visited many times. My family got
scattered to the winds during World War II. I grew up in
Colorado where I attended the Colorado School of Mines. I
was one of those Air Force brats. Ah! You don't want to hear
about that. I'm getting off the subject."

As the ranger started to wind up his talk, his eyes slid around
the crowd. They slipped over the young girl; a petite young
thing with eyes like the sky and hair as black as his own. His
eyes started to slide away. Did he really see what he thought he
saw? His eyes snapped back. His speech went on like a recording,
but his mind was thinking. *My God! She's coming on to me as I'm
standing here!*

Then Sunny's tongue slowly slid sensually back across the inside
of her upper lip. His speech stopped as he looked back at her
again. He hoped it was at a place where he was supposed to stop.

Sunny, realizing he was looking at her intently, showed a
question of surprise in her eyes. Then she remembered what
she had been doing and turned a deep red. Lord! Did he
think I was flirting with him in front of this group? These will
be the people I work with all summer. What a way to start the
summer off!

Bran blinked; visibly his mind came back to the group. "Any questions before I turn this meeting over to Art Brennen. He's the Trail Boss. We would be a complete wilderness without him around here."

He ran his hand through his crisp, black hair. His black eyes flashing as he started over to the group he'd been sitting with. He got an intense look from the head ranger as he sat down. Bran's mouth gave a quirk, "You'd better give that talk about no fraternizing between the sexes. I just got the biggest 'come-on' I've seen in public. She looks like trouble unless we nip it in the bud."

The head ranger chuckled, "Lucky dog! You bachelors get the come-on's, while us old fogies just ogle the young ones and wish we were young bucks again."

Bran raised his eyebrows slightly. "Well, it's not really my thing. I don't have time for these summer flings and during the winter I'm busy putting all the information together."

Taking the sting out of his words, Bran quipped, "Besides, there's only you old married codgers and your beautiful wives left then, unless you'd care to share them?"

The young ranger got a hard slap on the leg as the head ranger waited his turn at the lectern.

Sunny was still fuming over the look the Park Naturalist had given her. She watched him as he went over to sit down with the rest of the rangers. Tall, dark and handsome described him, but a crass ass was what he was, thought Sunny. I wonder if he really thought I was flirting with him or am I really putting my ego in high gear to think he would even notice me in this crowd?

The trail crew foreman finished his talk and turned the meeting over to the head ranger for the wind-up of the orientation meeting.

Sunny's eyes strayed past the head ranger and locked with coal black ones. Yikes! He's looking at me! Well! Let's see if he really did think I was flirting with him. She deliberately softened hey eyes and sensually ran her tongue along her upper lip.

Bran's cheeks reddened slightly and he quickly looked away.
Damn! She was doing it again and he had played right into
her hands. Now why had he even given her a second look? He
usually didn't give a hoot, and never had before. Fun was
something he hadn't had time for since his college years, before
Vietnam.

Sunny smiled to herself, her deep funk over with. I really
got to him that time, the pompous ass. The 'red man' turned
red.

Sunny wondered why she felt so good about getting the
best of the man. She usually never flirted with anyone. She was
just friendly with everyone; Sunny by name and sunny by nature.
However, rather stupidly, she had missed most of the last speech.
She hoped it wasn't anything she hadn't heard before. She'd
been to previous orientation speeches every summer she'd
worked for the Park Service. It was easy to let your mind wander.

The head ranger dismissed the meeting. The group started
to mingle exchanging names and identifying themselves with
their jobs.

The rest of the day was spent in a First-Aid class, the start of
many mini classes for the new crew. Tomorrow would be fun.
Fire fighting usually ended up in a water fight. Tonight was a
potluck dinner put on by the wives of the permanent
employees.

The wives of the rangers had set up a buffet table. Cold
pop and beer were in chests full of ice. Hot coffee permeated
the air and mingled with the other delicious smells of casseroles,
cold salads and bread. The wives were really good cooks from
years of exchanging recipes and performing these duties many
times before. Again there was a short introduction. Sunny knew
some of these wives and children would become her good
friends before the summer ended. She had many friends in
Stehikan from her previous work with the Park Service.

Sunny picked up her paper plate and a package of plastic
tableware, complete with napkin. "Nice little packages," she
murmured and started around the table, putting portions of

casserole, salads, pickles and bread on her plate. The bread smelled so good, must be homemade, she thought.

She gravitated to a corner with a couple of other girls. In the exchange of names and jobs, she learned they would be backcountry rangers like herself.

Again, like herself, Beth and Stacy were both petite. Did the top brass think only petite girls could be backcountry rangers? The girls laughed over this knowing their height wasn't on their resumes.

"How did you ever find this place to put your names in for a job? This is the back of beyond," said Stacy, a vivacious, beautiful girl showing her black ancestry off to an advantage. "I'm from California. Our neighbor worked up here one summer and loved it, so that's how I heard about it. How about you guys?"

"I'm from back east," replied a quiet spoken Beth. "I got my job through the Congressional Referral Program. You may get a job when you apply, but it can be any place there is a National Park. I'm still so tired from the flight out here, I'm fuzzy headed."

"Not quite!" laughed Sunny as she playfully tugged on Beth's straight, blonde hair, "I'm the native. I graduated from Eastern Washington University. I've taught kindergarten classes for two years just down the road from here in Everett. I've worked for three summers in the Parks. This will be my fourth. I was over at Stehekin, just across the mountains, loved it there, but felt I should try other places for experience. I barely got the last paper corrected complete with smiley face stickers on them before I had to show up here. I'll have to go straight back to teaching the minute I'm through at the end of the summer. I guess I'm the old lady here."

Sunny put her hands up along the side of her shirt like she was pulling suspenders. "Stick with me kids and I'll show you the ropes," she nasalled in her best W.C. Fields voice. The girls laughed. "I guess we'd better mingle," she finished.

Sunny turned to find the garbage can to dispose of her

plate. Turning a little too fast, she stumbled slightly and bumped into a brick wall in Park Service clothes. Quick hands came out to steady her. Sunny looked up into steely, black eyes.

"Hey man! I'm sorry," she breathed and her eyes widen as she realized it was the Park Naturalist. "I'm Summer Day, shortened to Sunny by some. I know that's a ridiculous name but my parents were of the flower children era, so I feel lucky it wasn't worse," her lovely mouth rambled. Her mind said you fool! *Shut-up! You're babbling!*

Black eyes looked down into blue; "I'm Bran Donovan." He held out his hand, but not a crack appeared in his armor.

Sunny daintily took his hand in a facsimile of a handshake. "I'm glad to meet you," and nervously that traitorous, dainty, pink tongue came out and sensuously found the spot where beginning of her cold sore was. Bran watched that tongue and his eyes turned to laser blasts that scorched Sunny.

"Stop that!" he hissed, and stalked out of the building. As he left, he faintly heard, "What did I do?" murmured a startled Sunny.

Sunny and most of the other summer people helped with the clean up. It was rather fun to mingle with the wives, and exchange banter with some of the children. The atmosphere was like an old time social gathering with all the wives, their husbands, and kids, the summer men and women, all helping clean up. But! Never a sign of the black eyed Bran Donovan.

Bran stalked back to his motor home. In place of having to find housing during his stint of duty doing research at each park, he'd found this thirty-three foot motor home ideal. He either parked it in a mobile home park or on the ranger station if it was set up for one. He paid a nominal grounds rent fee no mater where it was, but at least he didn't have to pack each time he moved. At Marblemount, he was able to park it at the station near the crew quarters.

It was a short walk from the meeting building. Not nearly long enough for him to cool down. This was a joke on him and it made him furious. He really needed to cool down, like in a cold shower. What the heck was the matter with him? He hadn't reached the ripe old age of thirty-seven to be having the *hots* for a snip of a young thing. He and the fellows could joke all they wanted to about getting rid of the old lady for a younger chick, but he didn't really approve of robbing the cradle.

He'd seen too much of that in Vietnam; Young girls selling themselves for anything, just to stay alive; Fellows taking advantage of those same girls, sometimes leaving them pregnant to fend for themselves after they had gone home. It made him sick of the human-race, and that was before he'd been captured and found out what inhuman really meant.

He reached the motor home and slammed the door. Not putting the lights on, he sat down heavily in one of the two easy chairs in the small living area. His hand automatically picked up the guitar that was always waiting for him. He closed his eyes and leaned his head back. His fingers strummed the guitar lightly, soothing his jangled nerves, slowly, cooling his libido and his temper.

Thinking of Vietnam cooled him totally. He very seldom consciously thought about those days. It brought back the nightmares. The Veteran's Hospital hadn't quite removed them all. Hell! He was going to have nightmares anyway. The minute he thought of Vietnam, they started coming back.

He'd been a pilot like his father before him. At the end of the war, he'd been shot down on a rescue mission with the copter. Two of his men had been shot as they tried to get away from the burning copter. He had been near death from his wounds but a fourth fellow, a medic, had been patching him up even as they were taken prisoner by the Cong. In the three years of captivity that followed he'd wished he had died. The beatings, the horse-like work, plus all the operations they'd done on him just to keep him alive were beyond description.

During a prisoner exchange, he'd gotten out. Months of therapy followed, although at that time, he felt he didn't need it. Therapy had never stopped the nightmares. His body was a scarred up mess from the injuries, beatings and torture. Then those later years while at the mining school, he'd never let anyone see the scars. He would wear shorts and roll up the sleeves of his T-shirts, but even he couldn't stand the sight of his eaten away stomach and back splayed with scars.

He'd finished his schooling at the Colorado School of Mines; a tough school, anything to keep his mind busy. His family had been very supportive. His dad, an ex-pilot, hadn't fared any better in his war having been shot down in a German attack and wounded.

His mother had been his father's nurse at that time in England, leading up to their marriage later. His dad had been able to take part in teaching young pilots until he retired.

He, himself, couldn't stand the thought of being in the military, yet here he was in a uniform again. This work he loved. It took him out into the lonely solitude. Sometimes he felt he must be a throwback to the Indians of old.

He'd heard stories about his mother's people. How they would go off wandering for months, then come home to tell stories of their travels. He'd never run into much prejudice. Of course, he'd never lived on a reservation or really done anything like his ancestors. Fishing and running were the closest he came to the old ways. His ability to survive in the wilderness was more from all the military training. Although, he had love it to start with, that was about all he could say he liked about the military now.

In all this mess of his later life, he'd stayed away from dating; or even close friendships. He always seemed to be with a group or else alone. He liked it that way.

He got a lot done in his work. Now, what made him get so uptight tonight? He could have ignored that sexy character if he'd wanted to.

What made her so special? She turned him on that's what. Why, he hadn't been turned on by anyone or anything in so many years, he'd forgotten what it was like. Hell! He hadn't even screwed in a light bulb. His thoughts made him smirk. Maybe he should start with a light bulb. Now he almost laughed.

Things were looking up. He glanced down at his lap. Oh yeah! Now he did laugh; a real deep wonderful one. It was a sound he'd almost forgotten.

What was her name? Sunny Day, what a name and hair like midnight! Her lips were soft with a sensuous cleft in the lower one. He'd heard of leg men and men who liked busts, but who ever heard of a mouth man? Along with his thoughts, his hand picked out different cords on his guitar to go along with his mood, almost like composing music to a thought.

His hand was now picking out a tune he couldn't remember the words to, and his rich baritone voice unconsciously hummed along. His body slowly relaxed. "*Night and day, you are the one. Only you beneath the moon and the sun . . . .*" This song he was humming was an old Cole Porter song his father had sung so well. He hummed but still no words came to mind, they were just outside his sub-consciousness. But they would come to him eventually.

CHAPTER 4

DISCOVERS POTTERY PIECE

Sunny was loping along the densely timbered trail. A startled squirrel chirped in the trees. She had disturbed him. Her long hair flipped back and forth. The flipping was unconsciously planned as it both cooled her scalp and kept the flies away.

After two days in the backcountry, it would be good to get to Ross Lake Guard Station to shower and sleep in a bed, thought Sunny. The backpack began to pull so she slowed to a fast walk. She usually didn't run with a backpack, but that last stretch of trail with its slight decline was just right. It eased the jarring effect of walking. Ahead, up a sharp incline through the dense trees, the skyline lightened. There would be a terrific view of Ross Lake and the surrounding mountains mirrored in it.

Her boots made a clumping sound as she passed over a log bridge. The water, traversing a ravine, was shadowed, gurgling over the moss covered rocks edged with ferns and giant boulders. It was wonderfully cool here and eased her sweating body.

Sunny broke through the timber into the clearing. Shasta Daisies covered the field in a summer shower of snow-white blossoms. Purple Lupine provided a sharp contrast. Later, the Indian Pain Brush would bloom making the meadow a flag of colors floating over the grasses. How many times had she sat in a meadow like this imagining building her vacation cabin in it? The clearing was reasonable large for this area. She supposed it had been made by an ancient forest fire. A small alpine creek meandered down through the moss and grasses. Its path determined by the rocks in its path and the slope of the land.

Sunny picked a collection of rocks near the stream to slip her pack off, setting it back off the trail against them. She grabbed her insect spray and sprayed herself. The mosquitoes were fierce at this time of year.

She was thirsty. Usually the best water was closest to the shadowed trees, so she followed the stream a bit. That's strange! It seemed to come from under the cliff, with no visible source. Anyway, she was too thirsty to explore farther.

Sunny bent down to sip from a small rippling waterfalls. She cupped her hands several times to drink. Not too much water or she would get sick. Drink many times but not too much each time, those were the rules of a backpacker. It was also the rule to bring a water purifier with you now days to prevent Giardia, a parasite you could get from contaminated water. The water of the North Cascades was excellent and pure if it came from a spring like this water seemed to. Ah, that tasted so good, she thought.

Sunny turned around. "My god, what a view this is."

There was Ross Lake, with Jack Mountain reflected in the glacier blue of the water. Desolation Mountain was in the background. Farther back still, was Hozomeen Peak, the sentinel that marked the Canadian border. Pun'kin Mountain sat like a round vegetable floating in the middle of the lake. A few boats were coming down the lake. They looked like bugs on the water. Fishermen were going back to Ross Lake Resort, or maybe to Big Beaver Campground, where she had just come

from. You either walked a trail or boated to Big Beaver. No
roads were in this part of the backcountry.

"I could stay here all day. It's so beautiful," she muttered to
herself. You talked a lot to yourself when you were alone all day.
Sunny moved over slightly to a drier place and gracefully flopped
back in the grass. The huckleberry bushes hid her slight figure.
The tiny berries were green at this time of the year.

"It's so peaceful." Her hands gently caught at the water
flowing over the rocks. Just five minutes and she would be on
her way.

A small sound startled her awake.

"Darn! I went to sleep. You're not supposed to sleep on
the job." She quietly chastised herself even though this cliché
didn't hold true when your job wasn't a nine to five anyway.
She turned her head to see what had awakened her. A slight
rise of her head above the bushes; showed her a deer and twin
fawns. As the doe meandered, she ate a bit of scrub tree here,
a tuft of grass there. The fawns kicked up their heels and chased
each other.

It was all Sunny could do to lie there and not laugh at them.
Suddenly, the doe sensed danger, probably the scent of Sunny.
Her startled head looked around sharply. Seeing nothing
didn't make it right. She bounded out of the meadow,
obediently, the fawns followed.

Sunny struggled to her feet. She felt exhilarated, renewed.
These mountains and the air were a very healthful drug. She
started down the incline to get her pack. It was still a good
hour or so hike yet. A small, white object near the creek bank
caught her eye.

Half buried in the dirt and moss was a piece of pottery. It
looked like the bottom piece of a cup.

"Litter is found in the darnedest places." Sworn to protect
the wilderness, she laughed and slipped the piece into her
litterbag in her pack.

She struggled into her backpack and headed down the
trail. Her idle gone but not forgotten.

The day started as usual. Up and ready for action at eight the next morning. Sunny gathered with the others near the crummy, a van used for hauling a number of persons to the job site. You sat on the side bench seats and were able to put your equipment in the middle of the van kind of between your legs. It was uncomfortable as heck.

She wasn't scheduled for another hike yet, having just come off the fifteen mile one through beautiful, rugged country. Her two days off had rested her body. The time had been well spent at the Laundromat and replenishing her backpack for yet another long hike scheduled for next week. She would probably help check the campers in one of the campgrounds today.

Looking up, she saw Bran coming towards the crummy.

"He'll probably be our driver today," muttered Sunny to herself. Wouldn't you know she would get him? It seemed their paths crossed all the time. If she had to sit down, the only place would be near him, "And no wonder," still muttering, "he's such an old grouch," although no one else seemed to think so.

Leaning over once while sitting next to him, she had bumped his arm. If he could have looked any farther down his nose, he'd have been cross-eyed. She recalled how her arm had tingled. The fresh shaving lotion he used mingled with the heat radiating from her body. Strange reaction, she thought.

She took out her handkerchief and blotted her forehead and nose. It was going to be a hot one today.

As Bran reached the group, his eyes wandered over them. God, he was getting old. They looked like a bunch of little kids and he was their Scout Master. And . . . there she was! Couldn't he ever get away from her? His body was heating up just knowing she was there.

"Okay! I'm your driver today. I have a list where everyone will be dropped off, however, I need someone to work with

me today. It won't be hard work or brainy. Just a warm body will
do, able to hold a rod upright."

There was a murmur among the group. Everyone had a
job to do but Sunny. Their eyes settled on her. She shrugged.
Thinking of the hot sun, Sunny chirped, "I've got a very warm
body. Will I do?"

The group laughed!

Good Lord! Why did she say that? Open mouth insert foot!
"I mean. It's very warm out today. I've got nothing to do. Besides,
I may learn something to help my kindergarten class." Oh-h-h,
she wailed in her mind. Now, I've classed his job with the
kindergarten.

The rest of the crew, knowing Sunny thought Bran was an
old grouch, believed this to be a real joke on her and food for
the gossip mill tonight.

"Yeah, she can go," said one of the fellows. "Let her brighten
up an old mine." Bran groaned to himself. What started out to
be a good day, just turned into thunder and lightning, "Okay
Night, you'll go with me. Everyone in! Let's get this show one
the road."

And running true to form, by the time Sunny got in, she
had to sit in front with Bran. Sometimes, she thought, the crew
planned things against her, and if they did? Woe-be-unto-them,
she would get even.

The crummy traversed through the little town of
Marblemount and headed up river towards Newhalem, the
picturesque little mountain village at the foot of Gorge Dam,
owned and operated by the electric company of Seattle City
Light. The crew talked in monotone voices to each other for
the fifteen-mile drive.

Normally, Bran would never make small talk, preferring
silence to meaningless chatter. His years of stoic behavior were
hard to change and he'd never bothered to try before. Now
for some reason, he felt mean just sitting in the driver's seat,
looking straight ahead.

He had noticed this girl, sitting next to him, was usually

very animated. Now, she looked straight ahead, never cracking a smile. Pity he had that effect on her. She usually brightened his day a little, even if he didn't want to admit it.

"Well Night, do you think you can hold a pole while I take readings? I'm trying to find the exact location of this one digging marked on the claims map."

"Day! Sir, my name is Sunny *'DAY'*!" She leaned forward looking into his face as she emphasized her last name.

"Oh yeah! Sorry! Sunny Day," he said as he quickly glanced at her and then back to the road again. Now, why couldn't he remember her name was Sunny. Every time he came in contact with her, his mind registered '*Night*'. It was probably that black hair cascading down her back. That blue-black sheen was like a summer's moonlight night. Something you wouldn't mind getting lost in, run your fingers through—, eyes to the road, old boy, he reprimanded himself, emphasizing the O-L-D part.

Now that the ice had been broken, and she really meant '*ice*', she remembered something she needed to tell him about.

"Mr. Donovan, I've got something back at the station I thing you should see."

"Okay, Night, er-r Sunny, you can call me Bran. We're really not that formal in the Park Service. We end up being called whatever is more comfortable. For some, it ends up their last name, others their first and a few with nicknames, but no one is Mr."

Hearing him slip again, Sunny beamed her radiant smile at him. "Okay, Bran," said with emphasis, "and I'll let you call me '*Night*'."

For the first time, she got a beautiful baritone laugh out of him. The change in this taciturn man left Sunny with her mouth gaping. She had been having a tough time keeping her eyes off him all along. Now, she caught herself actually staring. Under that tough exterior was a beautiful man. Sunny felt she would sure like to find him again.

"Now, Night," receiving a sideways glance from Bran and a half smile, "what have you got that I need to see?" And I don't mean your *bod*, he thought, and why all these lecherous ideas when he never, but never, had these kind of thoughts?

Oblivious to this last Freudian slip, Sunny continued. "On the last trip out in the back country, I picked up a piece of a cup, I think, and it has *Holland* printed on it. I was about to pitch all of the garbage I had picked up, when I remembered that piece of pottery. You usually don't take glass things on a backpack, especially Dutch china, so I dug it out and washed the mud off. It was the bottom to an exquisite piece of Holland Delft. What do you thing?"

Mulling it over, Bran responded. "I think you're right. I should see your piece of pottery. There have been lots of glass and cooking utensils found around these old mining sites, but nothing like real china. Was there a homestead area close?"

"No, this was in a meadow on the side of Sourdough Mountain, kind of across the lake from Ruby Arm area. I haven't been out again to see if the area can be seen from the lake."

They had reached the first drop-off site for the crew cutting off further conversation between the two. Bran let the first of the crews off at Goodell Creek Campground.

They continued the drive on up the canyon towards Diablo where some of the crew would get off at Colonial Creek Campground. From Newhalem on, the canyon narrowed with cliffs so high they cut off the sun. Only pools were left in the riverbed far below. The dams were holding back all the water. A token amount went over one spillway of Gorge Dam to keep fresh water in the pools to insure that the fish stayed alive. The rest of the water went trough a tunnel to force water through the giant turbines, which ran the mighty generators that supplied electricity to the city of Seattle. Sunny kept quiet as Bran drove the twisting road traversing the narrow canyon, with its two rock tunnels. In one rocky area, Bran told Sunny that mountain goats came down in the winter to feed on lichen and be close to drinking water.

Having dropped of the rest of the crews at their designated work areas, they reached the parking lot at Panther Creek.

Here Bran and Sunny got out their daypacks and assorted gear. Bran handed Sunny some of the supplies they would need for the day. Bran led the way down to the bridge that crossed Ruby Creek. They started the hike that would lead them to their job for the day.

The day was going very well thought Sunny as she worked with Bran in her efficient way. He may have thought he was a little addle-pated with some of her foot-in-mouth sentences and the devil-may-care attitude she projected, but she knew she was a good worker.

Bran was impressed with Night. She never talked unless she needed to, but smiled a lot as she looked around, noticing the birds in the trees or a sassy squirrel running around. She wore her uniform with grace and her hiking boots were worn but well cared for. Her hair was in one long braid down her back. Her image was completely professional today.

While they were surveying, he often saw her face in the transit and had to remind himself to look at the leveling rod, or the flagging as it was placed. That cleft in her lower lip was doing things to him again.

They flagged the area until Bran decided this one spot was it, the site of one gold mining operation. Sunny looked around. There didn't seem to be any signs of a gold mining operation, but then, that was a hundred years ago. There was just enough space for a camp in the cleft of the rock cliff.

She had admired Bran's efficient work style all day. He wasn't so bad to work with. In this mood, she could almost like him. A lot! He was certainly good looking in a chiseled sort of way. But those snapping black eyes and that dark clean-cut look, those broad, strong shoulders—, Sunny had to blink her eyes back to the present. Lord, what was the matter with her? She was too old for this hero worship stuff. This was better left to her little kindergarten students.

Bran and Sunny explored a little. Bran showed her signs of a blackened rock wall where fires had been built. The moss and ferns had nearly taken over. The wall had reflected heat

back to the miner. Gold could have been found in the bend of
the river here, but no sign remained to tell the story except
the blackened rock and Bran's co-ordinates. He drove a
numbered brass spike into the ground and covered it with
dirt. If it became necessary, the spike could be found again
with a metal detector. Bran marked the numbered area in his
book, along with a description of the area.

They removed all the flags; red tape tied to trees and
bushes, and went to pick up the rest of the crew for the trip
home.

CHAPTER 5

ROSS LAKE

A few days went by before Bran had time to think about Night's piece of pottery. Tonight the crew would be having their regular volleyball game. Night was always there if she was in camp. She was very active. Bran thought he could do with a workout, too. After a steak supper cooked over a grill set up outside his motor home, he felt good enough to tackle the volleyball court.

The crew was already slowly forming teams. As each person came, they would go to the side with the least people. As Bran appeared, one group let out a yell. "Whoopee! At last a tall person for our side!"

Bran good-naturedly loped over to that side. Sure enough, somehow, the mini-crew of backcountry rangers were all on one team. Because of their petite size, '*mini-crew*' had become the nickname for the backcountry rangers. For some strange reason, this years group were all short, three girls, all about five foot two or under and Bob, the only male, maybe five foot six at the most. Bran's six-foot height made him look like a giant. His good physical shape was from hiking the trails and jogging every morning at daybreak.

Bran had an instant flashback. Volleyball had been a Viet Cong prison camp game for those with enough strength left to play it. The game went well, both sides rather even in spite of size. On one spike, Bran had come down and found Night right under him. He had thrown his arms around her and they danced around a bit trying to keep their balance. She had felt so little and soft.

He couldn't remember, but he thought he had given her an extra hug before he had set her firmly, on her feet again.

The game wound down because of darkness. The words "Good game!" was being passed about. Bran looked around to find Night. He wanted to see that piece of pottery.

"Hey Night, could I see your piece of pottery before you turn in?"

A jovial quip from one of the crew was heard. "Is this the same as '*seeing your etchings*' Bran?"

"All in the name of business, guys," he chuckled.

"Sure Bran, I'll run and get it." Darn! She'd miss her shower or have a cold one, depending on the amount of hot water available. However, when she thought about that time he had his arms around her and that quick hug had nearly crushed her, her face burned. She could use the cold shower. Laughing gaily, as she was prone to do, she went to fetch the artifact.

Coming back out, she found Bran in one of the folding chairs he had set up by his motor home. As Sunny went over to him, he said, "Come on inside. The mosquito's will suck your blood dry if you sit outside even for a minute."

Sunny went up the one step to go in. It was really a beautiful piece of work, this motor home. Everything you could need was there and in it's place: microwave, TV, stereo piped to all the rooms, air conditioning, and the decor could only be called 'plush'. The colors were unusual; royal blue rug, white leather chairs, white oak walls and cabinets. Chrome and glass were abundant in accent pieces. White Venetian blinds covered the windows with a paisley print ruffle over each window. This again was picked up in the throw pillows both in paisley and blue velvet. It could have been a ship's cabin. A guitar leaned against one comfortable leather chair. Sunny took the other.

"Would you like something to drink? I'm having a cold beer, but I have pop also." He still thought of her as being underage to drink. Unknowingly, Sunny asked for a pop and got a diet 7-Up handed to her, confirming Bran's thoughts.

"Now, let me see your pottery."

They examined the piece. "This really does look like something I should investigate. Could you take me to the place you found it?"

"Sure, but when? I've got a hike ahead of me next week. My only free day will be this Wednesday or Thursday, my days off. Could you go on one of those days?" She gave Bran one of her usual smiles that would have brought most men to their knees, begging to go.

Bran wasn't much better and quickly took a drink of his cold beer. "Sure, Thursday would be great. You could stay over at the Ross Lake Guard Station when we return, so you would be rested up to start your week out."

Sunny was already missing her trip back with him and they hadn't even left yet.

Bran picked up a day-planner book. "Okay! Scheduled for Thursday; *A hike with Night.*" He inked that in and looked back up. "We'll take my car in case this turns out to be unofficial business, but I can haul your gear even if that sports job outside doesn't look capable. It really does have a lot of room where a back seat should have been."

Sunny agreed with the plan and left the motor home with a "see you later" exit line. It is doubtful if her feet touched the ground in the short distance it took to get to the crew quarters. Her head was in the clouds, her heart was pounding, and her fingers were counting the days to Thursday. "Whoopee!"

Thursday was a beautiful day in mid-July. High cumulus clouds floated in the cerulean blue sky with air so clear it seemed to magnify the beauty of the valley. Bran stowed Sunny's pack in the back of his Datsun 240Z sports car.

He had washed and waxed it. The black car was as pretty as the picture Bran got of Sunny as she came out of the door for the last time. Neither was in uniform. Sunny was dressed in her blue tank top and shorts, with a loud tropical printed camp shirt covering her arms that completed the outfit. The front tails of the shirt were tied in a knot on either side for no reason that he could see, but that it was stylish. Her long black hair was held back by a blue *'Alice in Wonderland'* band.

Bran had black cargo pocket shorts on and a white T-shirt with the sleeves rolled tight to his shoulders. Sunny had never seen his body due to uniforms, and what was uncovered was beautiful. Through his T-shirt his muscles rippled up his back, as he stowed the last of the things in the back of the vehicle and closed the lid. His arms and legs were very brown. She supposed it was his Indian coloring that did the very fine job of tanning his skin. She liked what she saw and told him so with a very big smile. "You look very handsome today."

Bran was visibly startled, but collected himself, and gave her one of his half-smiles. "You're kind of cute, too for a half-pint."

'Half-pint' would normally have been fighting words to Sunny, but the day was too nice to spoil.

"Come on Night! Let's go!"

The trip up to Ross Lake, along the North Cross State Highway, was spectacular due to the clear beautiful day, but uneventful. Bran and Sunny made small talk getting to know one another, a little about the crew and work, more about home and family.

Bran's dad had been in the R.A.F. in England. Bran was Irish and Indian. His mother's people were here in the Skagit

Valley. They had always been closer to her family mileage wise, than to his father's, for visiting back and forth. Before they had been married in England during World War II, Bran's mother had been a nurse and had helped nurse his father back to health from his war injuries. After they were married, Bran's father had finally been transferred to an U.S. base as an exchange instructor dealing with foreign duty for new recruits. Bran's dad was a big man with red hair, now turned white, with an accent that could only be Irish.

His mother was also tall and stately, with black hair and eyes as black as her son's. His folks were both retired now but still lived in Colorado. Bran considered his dad, his best friend after the Vietnam War. Bran was a loner, he confided to Sunny. This last was no news to her, as the whole ranger station knew that.

They reached the parking lot above Ross Lake, where a trail led down to the lake. Both experienced hikers, they prepared to put their packs on. Bran's was a small daypack, but seeing Sunny's larger pack that was to do her for a week, he quickly put that on, although he had to adjust the straps. Sunny gave him a hard look, but picked up his pack and adjusted his straps to her smaller size. Off they went, their boots making small dust clouds as they walked the trail. A mile below, Ross Lake reflected through the trees like a huge aquamarine jewel.

Down at the lake on the floating guard station, they quickly exchanged packs, with Sunny removing a small fisherman's vest with many pockets. This she used for her daypack. She explained she had found it was ideal for her as the weight was distributed more evenly. The ten essentials of a backpacker fit neatly in the many pockets. The pockets in front allowed her to get things out as she needed them, without stopping to put the pack down and rummage around in it.

Bran had the food, so she had only to slip on the vest. She decided to fold her camp shirt and stick it in the back pocket of her vest. The weather was too warm to wear very much.

They left her other pack at the guard station, to be used later, for her weeklong hike in the backcountry.

There would be a good hour's hike to the meadow; maybe more as it was hot today and they didn't need to push themselves. They would first have to cross over the spectacular Ross Dam that held water back for twenty-six miles to the Canadian Border and beyond. Sunny found on the level areas, she couldn't keep up with Bran's longer stride, but uphill and down she did as well as he did. This time to her surprise, on the service road leading to Ross Dam and the trailhead, Bran took her hand. Doing this both helped her along and kept him to her pace.

Sunny couldn't believe this was happening. She gave him many glances, but never did he look down at her. When they reached the trailhead, he dropped her hand and let her get ahead of him. Without Bran's distraction, Sunny swung out in long strides, happy to be on the trail with the mountain breezes rustling the leaves, the smell of the trees on the hot summer's day, and the only sounds were their muffled footsteps.

Bran, on the other hand, was having a little trouble. It had been bad enough when he had grabbed her hand, but now he had to watch her shapely behind walking up ahead. Several times he caught his head swinging to the rhythm of those swinging hips; left, right, left, right. Damn! Maybe, he was getting to be a bun's man, along with eyeing her mouth all the time. Then, again, his hand was kind of weak from all the feelings it had gone through while holding her hand.

His attitude towards her had really done a flip. He found out on the drive up she wasn't a teenager, like she looked, and he wasn't a dirty old man, with some of his private thoughts he'd had about her. She was old enough to know her way around. Hell! She was probably more experienced than he was, considering he had left his wilder days behind, before Vietnam.

Up ahead, he could hear a stream. If it was close to the trail, he'd stick his head in it to cool his thoughts. The stream was coming off a low hung cliff. A pole bridge spanned the short distance where the stream flowed under it. Reaching out, Bran cupped water and threw it over his face and ran his hands through his hair.

"A little hot are we," she quipped. If only you knew, thought Bran.

"Would you like something to eat? It's about lunch time," Bran asked.

Sunny replied, "No, I'd rather eat in my meadow. It shouldn't be too far now."

About twenty minutes more brought them up to the high meadow. As Sunny had said, the view was terrific. The sweet pervasive smell of the mountain flowers wafted on the gentle breeze. Ross Lake's milky blue color came from the many glaciers melting into it bring with it the silt from olivine rock. The meadow was filled with all the colors of the flag now. The Indian Paintbrush flowers shown red and there was blue Lupine and white Shasta Daisies still left. If you looked closely, the huckleberries were forming into nicely rounded orbs.

They stopped for a minute to contemplate the view of the meadow and lake. Bran asked Sunny if she had heard the true joke about the glacier silt called *'flour'*.

"No I haven't. What could be a joke about that?"

"Well, it seems like a elderly lady came into the park office to ask why the Skagit River was so milky colored instead of the crystal clear water she had heard about, and wondered what we were going to do about it? The ranger on duty kindly explained to the lady that it was flour from the glacier waters flowing into the river. The lady thought for a minute and then said in a huffy manner, 'I don't see any blossoms on it,' and walked out of the office." Bran looked at Sunny with a smile in his eyes, while Sunny laughed at the foibles of the human race. She took Bran across the meadow to the meandering stream. At the stream, they walked up towards the rockslide. She pointed out the spot she had found the piece of Delft buried.

In the shade of a huge Douglas Fir tree, near the base of the slide, they removed their packs and went over to the stream to wash and cool down. The stream did come out from under the slide with no visible means of supplying the water except for the main creek down in the tree-lined ravine. They could hear a water fall farther back in the ravine. A diversion could bring water this direction, or a spring could be under the slide. After mulling it over, a spring farther back under the slide, was their consensus.

All supposition was done in small talk and general conversation. They went back to the tree and sat down among the soft fir needles. Bran set out the food he had packed.

They ate cheese sandwiches and hands full of Gorp: a mixture of small chocolate candies, peanuts and dried fruit pieces. When thirsty they drank their bottled water. Sunny had brought pre-sweetened Kool-Aid, which she mixed with her water. Bran scoffed. She ate her Gorp, one piece at a time, daintily picking out the goody she wanted each time. Bran laughed.

They discussed how they would explore this meadow, while they ate. The decision was to do it together, rather than separate. In preparation to leave, they cleaned up their lunch mess.

Hearing some squirrels scolding them from the trees, Sunny decided to leave her bread crusts and a few peanuts out for them. She put the food on a piece of tin foil used to wrap their sandwiches in. She would pick it up as they left the meadow, putting it in her vest to take out.

Bran didn't approve of leaving the food. He felt that wild animals shouldn't rely on humans for their food. He only mildly objected as he had been having too good of a time, basking in the sun and listening to her ideas. He would indulge Night this time, he thought.

They decided to start where Sunny had first found the piece of pottery, maybe they would find more. Nothing was found. They circled the meadow looking for signs of an old garbage dump, although Bran knew pioneers usually dumped everything down their outhouse hole. Over to one side they discovered a strange collection of stones. This could have been a primitive outhouse at one time, but also, fire fighters or hunters could have made it. It would need more equipment than they had with them to dig it out, if that was what it really was. Sunny gagged just thinking they might have to dig it out. Again Bran laughed. God, this girl was good for him. He had almost forgotten what his own laugh sounded like.

They studied the area around the slide. The slide must have happened years ago as the trees above the huge cliff were quite large. They worked their way around to the ravine again. It was too steep to explore there.

Bran decided to leave their packs under the big Douglas Fir tree awhile longer, then go down to the main trail and follow it to the bridge across the stream. They did that.

Looking from the bridge they could see no sign of the falls. The ravine went too far back to explore today, although you could walk on this side of the hill opposite the meadow area, maybe even as far back as the falls they could hear in the distance.

It was getting late, so they decided to leave it for another day. Maybe next time they would get an earlier start by staying over night at the guard station.

They went back to the meadow. In their absence, two ravens had been picking their packs looking for food or shiny objects, which ravens loved to collect. As they approached the tree, the ravens flew up into it. Seeing that Bran and Sunny were going to stop, the ravens took off flying across the meadow their raucous cawing could be heard at being interrupted.

They checked their packs to see if anything was missing. Only the tinfoil that held their sandwiches had been pulled apart. Sunny's food was gone, but she had put it out for the squirrels anyway.

Sunny began picking up her lunch trash to put in the

garbage bag she always carried. The motto: *'pack it in, pack it out'* forever stamped in her brain, made this an automatic act.

"My god Bran, look!"

There hidden by the tattered foil was another piece of pottery. This piece looked like part of a dish. The Delft pattern was imprinted on it. The ravens had been doing some horse trading when interrupted.

"Bran, if your people believe in anything, you know it's the symbol of the Raven. It's a sign Bran! There is something here some place." Sunny, fell into her usual habit of talking too much when she was excited. However, her prattle fell on deaf ears.

Bran just stared. He was in shock. Through his whole body, a creeping chill was developing. He actually shivered in this hot day. Come out of it! He chastised himself. This is just a piece of pottery. But he knew his mother's people would never think so. Bran wrapped the pottery in his handkerchief and carefully put if in a pocket in his pack. He then shouldered his pack, while Sunny put her vest on. She gave Bran several curious looks.

It was too late in the day to explore more, but both knew this wasn't the end. They would be back. Sunny didn't disturbed Bran's thoughts. He hadn't spoken a word since the discovery. 'Struck dumb' was an apt description, except Sunny knew there was nothing dumb about Bran. When he did choose to speak, all he said in a distracted voice was, "I'll have to get the old claim records out. I don't recall any mines close to here.

At the Ross Lake Guard Station, he thanked Night for the good day he'd had and preoccupied, started the hike to the car. Sunny looked after him rather forlorn and puzzled. She went in the station to shower and cook her meager supper. Maybe someone would come along to share it, or at least be company, but she told herself, she would tell no one about the events of today.

After Bran left Sunny at Ross lake Guard Station, she had plenty of time to think. She showered and fixed her supper of beef stew out of a can, buttered a sourdough roll to go with the stew, and took it all out on the deck to watch the sunset. She dangled her tired feet in the cold water as she ate. It felt good.

The rest of the crew would be coming in soon. Sunny knew that quite often Stan, the Ross Lake Guard, might stop to eat supper at Hozomeen, a campground at the upper end of the lake. Sometimes, he would picnic and visit with campers at campgrounds along the lake. As long as he had his radio communications close by it didn't mater what time he got to the guard station. Stan was a very experienced boater and could navigate even after the moon came up. Even to the experienced, navigating was dangerous, as deadheads, floating logs of debris were hard to see making the going slow. He usually preferred to get in before dark.

Sunny thought of Bran. She was finally beginning to like him a little. Their talk in the car today had been friendly and she knew a little more about him now. His dad sounded like a real winner, an exuberant fellow that Bran seemed to really like. She could understand that. She liked her own father, although was closer to her mother. She could confide in things to her mother, whereas she asked her father's opinion. He always had a ready answer to her questions.

From what she could deduce, Bran was just the opposite. He seemed to seek out his mother for answers. She was the quiet one. Bran must take after her, both in looks and personality, from what he had told her.

This had been a strange day. Bran held her hand! This may have been a simple act, but it had felt so good. How strange it was that after all the years of touching and hugging people at the commune where she had been raised, this one man made her have feelings she'd never experienced before. She'd had dates and talked girl-talk with roommates, but right at this minute, she realized she hadn't understood what they were talking about. Talk about your arrested development! She was the best example of it she knew.

She remembered the commune years. Her father had

started it more as a way to get away from the materialism of the
world at the time. People just started coming there. Clean
living was what her folks preached. Those on drugs; got off
with hard work on their part and a lot of encouragement. Her
dad had started job programs for anyone interested. Otherwise,
just daily survival, clean living and helping one another was
the creed. This creed made her what she was today; a very
protected, naive, nice person.

They raised their own fruit and vegetables. There were
cows for milk and butter, eggs from the chickens and someone
had even tried a few goats and sheep. By selling some of the
by-products from the commune, they were able to buy what
they couldn't raise.

Her thoughts came back to her day with Bran. He had
acted so strange after discovering that piece of Delft pottery.
She had been so excited and had been babbling away as usual,
when it finally dawned on her that Bran was acting spaced out.
After that, if it hadn't been such a beautiful day, the hike would
have been one big deep freeze.

Sunny's ears perked up. She turned her head to listen. A
boat could be heard coming down the lake, plus voices up on
the access road. The crew was about to descend on the guard
station for the night. It was lively in the evenings. There was
always some tale to tell about the campers, the animals, or even
a joke on themselves. Nothing was sacred when this bunch got
together.

Therefore, it wasn't so strange when Sunny said nothing
about the piece of pottery or the ravens. Her contribution to
the evening was only that Bran wasn't such a bad guy after all
and the hike around the lake was hot but beautiful.

The hike back up the hill for Bran was a silent one. There
may have been birds chirping their evening song or squirrels
hunting for an evening meal, but Bran just trudged along not
seeing or hearing, but deep in thought.

The ravens back at the cliff still had him under their spell. Bran was thinking; *it's strange how the raven kept appearing in his life.* When the helicopter had gone down in Vietnam and he had been delirious with his wounds, the thing that had awakened him was a raven flying towards him in his mind. The raven had nearly settled on his chest with its wings expanded. The spread of its wings must have been five feet, although, normally a raven wasn't that large a bird, nor frightening. It looked down at him, its talons on its feet extended to settle on his chest or grab out his heart.

Heart pounding, he had awakened before either could happen to the Vietcong standing over him and his own medic. Why the soldiers hadn't shot both of them dead like they had the other two men in his group, he would never know. The medic had been unhurt, it seemed at the time, but Bran had never seen him again to even thank him.

The raven had come to him many times later: after an operation, then again when he had been beaten senseless, and a great many times as part of his nightmares. It had finally come to mean it was time for him to wake up. He had always awakened just before the raven had landed.

Today wasn't like the rest of the times. He had been awake and curious to what the ravens had been into. It was when he had held that piece of pottery, his eyes had seemed to glaze over and the raven had come at him again. He could still feel the chill over his body just thinking about it. Was it time for him to wake up again? But why? What for? Why and what for, followed in his mind all the rest of the long drive back to the Ranger Station.

It was time for him to visit his Indian ancestors to find answers. The Raven was part of their heritage, so they would be better versed in the meanings it represented.

CHAPTER *6*

BRAN'S SECRET

Sunny and Stacy arrived back at the Marblemount Ranger Station a week later. Both girls were looking forward to sleeping in their beds tonight instead of on a foam pad in sleeping bags on the hard ground. Tomorrow would be spent cleaning their camping gear, airing the sleeping bags and generally just getting ready for the next trip out. In place of cooking supper, both girls chose to go to the Drive-In at Marblemount for a treat of hamburgers, French fries and a good, cold, thick milkshake.

They showered and changed into clothes other than their uniforms. Sunny drove them down in her Volkswagen.

"How can a person miss junk food so much?" drawled Stacy. "We had good wholesome food all week, but this milkshake tastes like nectar from the Gods!"

"I know," grinned Sunny, "but it also helps not to have to set up camp when you're already tired and then cook it yourself."

They drove back to the Ranger Station sipping on the

milkshakes, saving the hamburgers and fries to eat at the bunkhouse. They made a pitcher of lemonade from frozen concentrate, then sat out on the back steps of the bunkhouse to finish their meal. Some of the others were cooking their supper, so mixed smells wafted out the screen door. Sometimes the crew pooled their food for a potluck meal, other times they planned a meal and shared the cost. Still other times like today, Sunny and Stacy did their own thing. The main rule was to clean up after yourself.

After supper, as usual, the gravitation was towards the volleyball court. The vivacious Stacy was already stirring, and provoking everyone to get up. Her chatter made even the laziest one with a full belly move. Tonight, however, Sunny opted to stay where she was. There didn't seem to be any mosquito bent on blood sucking. Just a few bats flying around picking off any insect brave enough to fly around the evening sky. Actually, they kept the mosquito population under control.

Sunny could see a light on in Bran's motor home. His door was open with the screen door closed. His blinds were closed. Thinking, of the last time she had seen him, she wondered if he had ever got over his blue-funk. It was still strange how he had changed so after they found that piece of pottery.

"Oh well!" she sighed. She had done her part in showing him the location of the area to look around in. The rest was up to him.

She leaned back against the building, her legs straight out in front of her, and crossed at the ankles on the porch. The light in Bran's motor home went out. Now, there was nothing but the peace and quiet of the night. The volleyball players were yelling back and forth, but that was over by the fire warehouse. Sunny closed her eyes and listened to the evening's tranquil sounds.

From Bran's trailer came the first strains of a guitar being strummed. It slowly gained more volume as the player warmed up. Then the reverberations of a beautiful baritone voice issued

forth in a song. The song wasn't modern, but more of a song
you would sing to quiet a baby's fretting, or to sing to your
lover after a beautiful time together. The next song Sunny
heard was more of a humming. The player trying to find the
words to a song. It was a beautiful song, but the player got
frustrated and hit a discordant '*whang!*'

The trailer screen door slammed shut as Bran came out.
He had to walk right by Sunny unless he was going to play
volleyball. He wasn't, and as he seemed to be going past her
without speaking. Sunny spoke to him.

"That was a beautiful song you just played. I didn't realize
you were such an accomplished singer. That was just beautiful,
really beautiful."

"Oh! I'm sorry. I didn't see you sitting there, Night. There's
a song that keeps going through my mind all the time. I can
hum it, but I can't bring the words to mind. I'm sorry I disturbed
your evening. I thought everyone would be over at the volleyball
court or I wouldn't have played so loud."

"You didn't disturb my evening Bran, you really added to
it. I'd love to hear you play some more sometime."

Bran seemed embarrassed. "I usually don't make a spectacle
of myself, but we do have jam sessions every now and then over
at Art Brennan's house. He's the trail crew foreman."

"Yes, I remember him from the orientation meeting. I
didn't realize when I took the backcountry ranger job I'd be so
isolated from most of the people on the station. When I was at
Stehikan, I was in the information center, so saw everyone and
knew everyone."

"Don't you like your job?" asked Bran with concern in his
voice.

"Oh! Yes, I love it. I don't mind the isolation. I'm probably
more rested even with all the hiking, than I've ever been in
my life. It's just different is all."

The sounds of the volleyball game dissipating for the night
resounded back to the couple. In a few minutes, the crew came
by and "Hi, Bran" and other verbal quips were heard. The

group continued on into the bunkhouse. A few ruffled Sunny's hair as they went by.

Bran, after bidding her goodnight, he commenced his evening stroll. Sunny followed the crew into the bunkhouse to bed.

It was another hot day in July. If they didn't get rain soon, it would be one hell of a fire season, thought Bran. He had been in one big fire in California during a tour of duty there for the Forest Service. Even though the hazard pay was good, he sure hated that duty. Destruction of a beautiful forest, besides the hot, grimy, back breaking work made it miserable. All hands had been recruited to help otherwise, he wouldn't have been called in. It had even burned some exclusive, expensive homes.

Wiping sweat from his brow, he parked the pickup in its stall, wrote the mileage up in the vehicle's journal, and headed for his motor home. A good shower and a cold beer, then he'd write all those reports up he'd been saving for a rainy day. It didn't look like rain for a long time, so he'd better do them anyway.

As he opened the door, a blast of hot air hit him. How could it be hotter in here than out there? He thought. The air-conditioning switch was handy so he quickly turned it on. Maybe the beer first, then the shower, thought Bran as the air-conditioning started to cool the place down. Jeez, he was tired, and in the middle of the day, too. He plunked himself down in the white leather chair and slowly savored the cold beer.

Finishing the beer, he quickly threw the can in the recycling bin under the sink and swung back towards the bedroom and shower. "Ah! My kingdom for a shower," he mumbled. He quickly undressed, dropped his clothes to the floor and walked naked back into the bathroom and into a small cubicle shower. Stepping inside, he turned the water on. No water! Now, what the hell? Bran got out and checked the faucet at the sink, carefully not looking at his scarred stomach in the mirror. No water in the sink either. Well, no time to fuss now. He would shower and shave over at the crew quarters and come back and check out the water problem later.

He quickly pulled on a pair of clean jeans and grabbed a button shirt. Carefully, buttoning three of the buttons enough to cover his scars, and grabbing his shaving kit, plus a towel, now where were his shower shoes? Finding them he slipped on the rubber sandals, and headed out the door to cross the yard to the crew quarters.

Inside it was relatively cool. He hadn't been in here except to call someone out for duty, but a quick look showed him a rather large bathroom with several shower stalls, doors open to show no-occupancy, two sinks with long horizontal mirrors over them and a shelf for holding grooming gear. The toilets with doors were off to the other side of the showers. No one was around. Bran went in the shower stall. There was a place for clothes, so he stripped there and went on into the small, connected shower area. The water started out icy cold, but after the first shock, if felt good, and then started to warm. Bran kept the water to the cool side and finished his shower. Coming out, he dried himself with the towel and stepped into his jeans.

Leaving the towel around his neck, he went over to one of the sinks to shave. When he showered, he shaved with foaming cream and a razor. In between showers, he used the electric one he had. Today, he needed a lawn mower or weed cutter to get through this mess. He lathered his face and started a man's daily ritual.

Sunny, coming in the bunkhouse, heard the shower running. Boy! Did that sound good! Her day off in town hadn't been the great get-away she had hoped for. She hadn't found the new pair of boots she sorely needed. She would have to wait and go to REI, a recreational supply store in Seattle the next time she had her days off. She needed to visit her folks anyway. She smiled, wondering what new crusade they would be protesting.

Her parents had finally joined the main stream of life after the '*flower years*',but they still leaned to causes and always would. Her lawyer father still took the sad cases and won a lot of good causes with it. Her mother worked at a crisis center, and sometimes the only way Sunny could get to talk to her was to call there, even though it wasn't a crisis in her case.

The inherited money that had come from the death of both sets of grandparents, years ago, had never spoiled either one of her parents and it wasn't allowed to spoil Sunny either. In fact, it went for education and good causes. The farm, her parents lived on had been inherited by her father from his parents. It had been a commune by the time she had been born, but now, no one but herself and mother and father lived there. The area was slowly building up around them. Her folks sometimes talked about selling and getting farther away from it all, but their causes were always getting in the way and probably always would. Meanwhile, it was close enough for them all to commute to their respective jobs.

Dumping her purse in the locker, she stripped down and put her serviceable terry cloth robe on. She noticed in her locker mirror, the white of it made her tan show up. She slipped the 'Alice' band out of her hair and fanned her long hair out over the back of the robe. The terry cloth slippers were right beside the bed. She slipped them on her feet, grabbed the shampoo and her towel and off to the shower room she went.

Bran had just finished shaving and bent down to wash the rest of the lather off his face.

Bursting into the room, Sunny spied the person, presumably who had just showered, and with her usual, casual nature quipped, "Well, how's the water?" her momentum taking her almost up to Bran.

He straightened up in complete shock.

She spied his back. "Oh my god! What happened to you?" and as Bran turned to confront this intruder, she saw the terrible scarring on his stomach. She just stared.

"What the hell are you doing in here? Get out! Get out!" Bran yelled as he grappled around for his shirt.

"Don't yell at me, man! This is a co-ed place as if you didn't know and we usually wear clothes when we come in here!" Suddenly contrite, she continued in a caring voice, "Your scars! Oh, Bran! What happened?"

Turning on her like a viscous dog, "Shut-up! Leave me alone!" Bran yelled again, as he finally got his shirt on and stormed out of the room.

She heard the outer door slam so hard that others hearing it might have thought the volcano, Mt. Baker had erupted. Giving it some thought, as she got ready for a cooling shower. "Well, Mt. Donovan certainly had erupted," she mumbled. Just when they had finally started getting to know one another, this had to happen. The poor man! She knew he wouldn't want her pity though with those scars. He should have been dead from the wounds. A dead Donovan would have been more than she could have endured. Her heart ached just thinking about him, so mad, so hurt.

Finished showering, she toweled herself dry. She slipped into the bathrobe and slippers. Leaving the cubicle, she started to head to her room. Glancing around the bathroom area, Bran's shaving things and towel were still there. Sunny sadly picked them up, cleaned the sink a little for the next person, and headed for her room, meeting no one on the way.

In her room, she sat down on the bed. Her thoughts wandered. What to do, what to do? He's beginning to really affect me. I've just not given much thought to finding someone to love. In the commune, you loved everyone in a friendly sort of way. Love was just a nice word. It's starting to mean something totally different now. It's a tingling if you touch each other, a quickening of the stomach muscles if you see the person unexpectedly. There is a radiant feeling running down your length if you're spoken to. And sitting here, thinking about Bran, makes me want to hold him and kiss the hurt away. To the impulsive Sunny, the thought was as good as the deed. She jumped up and donned a pair of khaki shorts and her '*Banana Republic*' shirt. Then sorting Bran's shaving gear from her own stuff, she grabbed up the towel and his gear and headed for Bran's motor home.

Fuming Bran stormed back to the motor home. Even as he went, he knew it wasn't her fault. It's the same old hang up. No one! But no one sees his battered body, not even his nurse for a mother. Only the nurses and doctors at the VA hospital had evaluated him. He could have had skin grafts for his stomach, but the thought of more hospitals at that time had been abhorrent.

Time really was a healer and maybe now was the time for the plastic surgery, and time to lay his nightmares to sleep forever. Maybe, he was still blaming himself for living when so many had died. Maybe, he had wanted the scars to keep reminding him as a kind of penance. Maybe, he'd better get his butt over there and apologize to Night.

Thinking of her blazing away at him for yelling at her brought a smile to his face. It was so seldom that he smiled, most people would have checked to see if his face had cracked. Maybe, just maybe, life was on a roll and he would feel again. Feelings hurt, but lately other things were coming alive and they didn't hurt. In fact, they were so pleasurable he wondered how he could have forgotten them.

He could look around and see other women and never even give them a thought. Then in a sea of faces, one sassy little girl stood out with her sexy, kiss-able mouth and his whole world had changed, or should he substitute libido for world. Well, get over there and tell her you're sorry, you ass, before you slip back into your shell again.

Sunny, walking quickly across the yard before her courage failed, got almost to the motor home when Bran opened the door to come out, nearly smacking her in the face.

"Oh Bran!" but Sunny was interrupted as Bran said at the same time, "Oh! Hi Night. I was coming to find you. Please come in where it's cool. Please?" he ended with a solemn plea, his beautiful voice reverberating through Sunny.

She quietly stepped in and sat down in one of the leather chairs, putting the shaving stuff on the table next to the chair.

Bran automatically got a diet 7-Up drink out of the refrigerator, snapped it open and gave it to Sunny. After a quick deliberation, he took another one for himself. Keep a clear head, he thought, this is going to take all the courage I've got.

"Now Night, you deserve an apology and an explanation."

She tried to interrupt, but he waved her down and continued as he sat down in the other chair.

"I'm so sorry I yelled at you. That was your territory and I was out of line. These scars are from Vietnam. The back scars are beatings we all endured in prison camp. The front one was where I was wounded. It got infected. They cut away parts; several times, and I lived in spite of them. My body is perfectly healthy now, but I bear the scars of war. I've never let anyone see them; my family, the guys at school, no one but the doctors and nurses. I've crawled into a shell where nothing can touch me. We had to learn to do that in POW camp to keep our sanity."

He took a drink of his pop, his courage flagging. "It's only lately I've realized what a real loner, and impossible ass I've been. I'm changing. This metamorphosis seems to be happening since I met you. I really did enjoy our day on the lake. I'd hate for us not to be able to do it again because I'm such a nut case, but I would appreciate it if you didn't mention the scars to other people yet. As you have seen, I don't handle my injuries very well."

Bran stood up and leaned against the counter between the kitchen area and the living room. He gave Sunny a slight smile as he wound down. Sunny stood up. He towered over her in the small confined area. She was appalled at what Bran had gone through. How should she handle this touchy situation?

"Hey, big fellow," Sunny quipped, trying to lighten the mood. "Don't worry about me telling anyone. Your scars don't bother me. They are not the man I've gotten to know over all these weeks. The only scars we have to worry about are the scars in your mind, and I'll help you any way I can to get rid of those. Oh, Bran! You've got so much going for you. Your brain is sharp and I think you've got a beautiful body. You have a great sense of humor," now that you've let it go a little she adds to herself.

"And, my god that voice of yours makes my toes curl when I hear it. Besides, you've got great buns!" And Sunny giggled slightly as she stepped up and put her arms around him. Her hands patting his rear as she half hugged him.

Bran groaned at this tiny, beautiful girl's show of affection. He loved it, and he thought he might be beginning to love her. He just realized that all these sexual urges weren't just that, but the opening up of a whole new life. Life after Nam? Damn!

Damn had just taken on a whole new meaning. Cool it, Bran! He thought. This is all too new yet. Think it out. Taking his cue from this wonderful girl, he said, "Hey there, Night. I didn't know you were a buns girl," and gave her a gentle hug, then set her back to look into her eyes. What he saw was a very honest person looking back at him.

Slowly, a twinkle started in her deep shadowed pools. "But I knew you were a lip man the first time I saw you."

And right before his eyes, that little tongue came out and slowly ran across her upper lip. Yep! She sure had his number.

"And the thing you didn't know was that I had a cold sore starting just there, and I was NOT deliberately doing it." Her tongue stopped at a spot on her lip.

"Really? Right there you say, huh? Let me see." Sunny raised her face up so Bran could get a better look at it. Bran's face came down slowly to look at the area Sunny had indicated. His hands came up to cup her exquisite face. He brought his lips down in a slow sensuous kiss.

The kiss might have been long or short. The participants couldn't have told you. Inertia slowly took Sunny over, as the warmth of his kiss worked it's way down from her lips to her breasts; from her hardening breast to the very heart of her being where it balled up like a tornado before spreading to the insides of her legs. She could feel Bran hardening against her. He was not unaffected by this kiss either, she thought.

Bran slowly lifted his head and looked down at Sunny. She was completely relaxed, her eyes closed, her mouth slightly open.

"Is it better?" Bran quietly murmured.

Slowly coming out of her inertia, Sunny sighed, "Huh, better?"

"Yeah, your cold sore, is it better? I kissed it to make it better."

Now, really coming out of her kiss-induced coma, she quipped back, "So that's what you were doing! Kissing it better?"

"Uh huh! That's it." Bran breathed the words out quietly.

"Well, if that's the case, I've got a hurt by my neck, one on each eye, the tip of my nose and another cold sore starting," she answered him mischievously pointing at her lips, "here."

"Whoa little girl! Didn't you hear the speech on no fraternizing among the personnel while on duty?"

"Why, no I didn't. When was that?" Was it on one of her days off?

"It was at the orientation meeting. I saw this little snit of a thing rolling her luscious tongue at me and suggested to the Head Ranger that he should give his famous *'No fraternizing'* talk."

"Did you now! And I was so busy seeing if a certain pompous ass thought I was flirting with him, I missed the whole thing. I always wondered what I had missed. It seems it wasn't a thing that was important."

Backing off a little as things were getting a little out of hand for Bran, who had been out of circulation for so long, he said,

"Now, Night, I have lots of reports to do and I'm on duty yet, so why don't you get your cute little butt out of her while I do them and then I'll take you out to dinner at one of the local restaurants for being a good girl." His smiling face and quick pat on her behind took the sting out of his dismissing words.

Sunny smiled back at him, her eyes twinkling, "Okay big boy, you're on. About sixish, maybe?"

"Sure, that would be about right. I've got to fix the water to this rig too. See you then."

Sunny walked back to the crew bunkhouse. Her feet, that had dragged over this ground not an hour before, never touched the ground on the way back. At the bunkhouse door, Sunny saw the faucet where Bran's water was attached, and deftly turned the water on, making sure he would have no excuse for being late for their date.

And Bran, back at the motor home, was thinking, Man! I feel good. Where did that burnt-out go, and all the hurt and pain he was feeling? I feel great, just great! And absent-mindedly humming, *"Night and day, you are the one,"* he settled down in the area he had set aside for desk work and proceeded to up date his reports on the mine locations.

CHAPTER 7

FINDING THE CAVE

Bran was again on the west-bank trail on Ross Lake headed for the area where Night had found the pottery piece. It was a workday but Bran felt justified in going there by the events of this last week. The day was overcast. The mountains were shrouded in clouds. It was a good day to hike. Rain still wasn't in the forecast.

Bran had done his homework. The area where Night had found the pottery was not listed as a mining area. He had even gone to the county court house in Mount Vernon to see if the Park Service had missed a listing. There was none. He really didn't have a good reason for going back to the area. It was his gut instincts that told him to.

That, and the two days he had spent with his relatives. He had taken Tyson Tubbs, who was working on the history of the Indians of the North Cascades, with him. His relatives and their friends had been a great help. Just a quick call to one of his aunts had produced a potluck dinner at the lodge-house down at the reservation. Only a few of his relatives lived on the reservation, but it had only taken a *beat on the drum*, so to speak or the telephone in this day and age, to round up quite a few of them. Many of the people there were just friends and only slightly known to Bran.

After dinner, Bran informed them that Tyson Tubbs needed to know some of their folklore and any other interesting stories then might have to tell. They had been reticent at first, but Bran had started the story telling by relating to them about his Raven. He had never told the story before. The whole group had realized this was not a *funny* story and had rallied around him like a wolf pack protecting their cub. He had been treated to an Indian psychological work-up, much like the VA Hospital did, only dealing with his Raven, not the war atrocities.

They had told story after story about the Raven. This was the older people. The younger group had been as enthralled with the stories as he had been. A few of the younger group had told stories similar to Bran's, making him realize he wasn't a freak. One fellow said a wolf had stepped out in front of him and had slunk away. He found out later, he would have fallen over a cliff if he had crashed through the brush up ahead.

Tyson Tubbs had been delighted with the stories, plus had made contacts to talk with some of the old-timers at a later date.

Bran, himself, had enough information to know he had to pursue the lead the pottery had given him.

Raven was the creator. Raven let the light shine on the earth by breaking a hole in the sky. Raven played tricks on people by taking things from them, but what he left in its place was more valuable if you were smart enough to figure it out.

At the end of the evening, several relatives had given him talismans to carry with him; a lucky rabbit's foot, a squirrel's tail, a bear claw, an elk's tooth, and believe it or not, a raven's feather. He wasn't the only one to look to the Raven for guidance.

Bran's session, the next day with his Great-grandfather

Moses, was a highlight to Tyson Tubbs. Old Moses had been a shaman to the tribe in his later years. In his younger years, he had been such a hell-raiser he had needed a *spirit* to take care of him. He was nearing a hundred years of experiences, but what rang loud and clear to Bran was his need to trust this guiding *spirit*. Old Moses was adamant about that.

They hadn't stayed long with Moses as he tired easily. His one hundredth birthday in late August would be a huge event with half of Skagit County attending it. Bran's family would be coming up from Colorado for the celebration. Bran was looking forward to seeing everyone. He could hardly wait to introduce Night to them.

That thought made him stop and take note. Why in hell would he want them to meet Night? Bran looked around. He was still on the trail. He hadn't fallen over a cliff with his mind on his thoughts instead of the trail. In fact, he was at the place where he had soaked his head under the small waterfalls the last time he had been there. He grinned to himself as he remembered his thoughts at that time.

God, she had a cute butt! Just thinking about that day made him turn and splashed water over his head again. Oh, that felt good and so did his memories about the girl. No wonder he wanted his parents to meet Night.

She was waking him from a dark sleep time in his life. His mother would love her just for that. His dad would pick her up in a big bear hug and kiss her silly. AND wouldn't Night be surprised at that. Bran could feel himself getting jealous of his own dad and this was all in his mind, not in real life. Could he really be feeling life again? If he did, would he get hurt again?

Hell! Women had never hurt him. He'd been too young and empty headed to be hurt by women all those years ago when he'd last been with one. In fact, he had probably hurt them and hadn't given it a thought. The girls were just a good time in those days, much to his chagrin now.

"Oh, how the young doth hurt each other in the name of fun." He murmured having just invented his own quote. At his age he must be careful of Night. If he put the make on her, she would have marriage in mind? And was he up to marriage and a family?

Before he could delve into these weighty thoughts, he was at the meadow where they had found the pottery. Bran's mind immediately switched back to work.

He made his way up the meandering meadow stream. He wanted to check the area for anymore signs of civilization. Except for a gum wrapper that he put in his daypack, there wasn't anything. The meadow's grasses were starting to ripen so it had taken on a golden hue. It still was filled with wild flowers. The heavy, muggy air had a perfumed smell about it. A real storm was brewing. Each day a few more clouds came in, but usually burned off by late evening. If might not do so today.

Bran followed along the edge of the draw banking the meadow down to the main trail. He intended to get to the falls today but it wouldn't be on this side of the ravine. He followed the main trail through the woods and across the bridge to the other side of the creek. There, he left the trail and started traversing the hillside through ferns, moss and trees. It was so beautiful here, although dark from lack of light. The overcast day didn't help either.

About a quarter of a mile back up the stream, Bran came upon the falls. He had been keeping a steady pace and was almost at the top where the water broke over the edge of the rocks. It wasn't a large fall and was split in the middle by a huge rock. The other side of the falls rolled off the rocks into pools.

Now to find a way across unless he wanted to get his feet wet. Sure enough, farther up the creek windfall trees had spanned the small ravine. He took out his hatchet and knocked a few rotten limbs off the log he was crossing on. Nice bridge, he thought.

On the other side of the creek, the same side as the meadow was on, the going was rougher. He had to work his way along the hillside over rocks and around trees as large as three feet through. At the head of the falls, it was surprisingly level. The area on this side had a small beach of sand and pebbles where the water swirled before working its way down the falls into pools.

Ever mindful of his job, he looked around to see if any mining might have been in this area. Nothing upstream had indicated anything but virgin ground.

Now, as he looked around, a natural path seemed to wind down towards the area where the meadow was. The meadow wasn't all that far away when viewed from this angle. He started to follow the path. It was moss-covered and narrow; probably a deer trail. He came to a place where a small dirt slide had come down. Again, he took out his hatchet and scooped out footholds for himself.

If the deer could do it, so could he. The terrain was steep and with one false step he would fall into the creek below. Ahead, the creek angled away from the meadow, but was still a rock-strewn ravine. Bran kept to the narrow trail, taking care with each step. He was almost to the meadow area, but at higher elevation. Ahead the trail stopped at the huge face of the cliff where the rockslide was. He could see the deer trail has gone up and over the cliff top at this point where he was now. There was more dirt, ferns and trees around here with solid rock up ahead.

Going to the top of the cliff, he found he could follow the deer trail back to the meadow much easier this way, than the way he had come in from. He wanted to see what was at the end of the trail he'd been on so he went back down there. He could see it continued even though the deer didn't use that part.

On the original trail again, he slowly worked his way through the rocks and around another large boulder. This was a nice spot about five feet square. The sheer cliff he leaned up against circled around to the front where the meadow was. The Douglas fir tree he and Night has sat beneath was about twenty feet away. He was about fifteen feet up, but the rockslide went straight down to the ravine here. The stability of the rocks at this point was precarious. He'd still have to backtrack to go over the cliff when he went home.

No problem! This was a good place to rest and eat lunch. The grass was dry here. A clump of brush and ferns lined the rock he had just edged around. He eased his daypack off, got out his foil wrapped sandwiches and a can of pop, plus his apple. Washington's Delicious apples were something he could hardly get enough of.

As he ate, he looked the area over. Could there ever have been any mining here? He started looking for clues out of habit more than anything. A disturbance by the ferns and brush revealed a marmot. He threw a piece of apple towards the area. The shy marmot eventually grabbed it and ran off over the boulder and on up the trail. A marmot hole would be back behind the boulder.

Bran looked up towards the cliff front where an overhang of solid rock was. A strange discoloration caught his eye. Could that be traces of and old smoke trail up the round face of the rock? His lunch forgotten, his heart rate doubled with excitement, Bran jumped to his feet. With his hand on the rocks of the slide area, he leaned out to get a closer look.

At this point he looked straight down into a rock chimney. A real honest-to-goodness chimney! What he couldn't see sitting down, was as clear as day now that he knew what he was looking at. He was almost dizzy with excitement.

The smoke from the chimney would have come up, hit the rock underside and dispersed on the face of the rock cliff. With the ferns and trees up above taking the smoke, a fire would have been impossible to see. Still leaning over the rocks, he removed a few that had come down from the slide. Now he was able to see the shape of the chimney. He had found something: something very exciting!

But what? Miners usually didn't build chimneys or use Delft china. The slide had covered any entrance to whatever was down there.

The marmot hole! Maybe it led down there. Unheeding any lessons not to disturb the growth in the National Park, Bran leaned over the ferns and rashly pulled and tugged to remove them. A few slashes with the trusty hatchet got rid of the brush. In the corner between the cliff and the large rock was a hole about a foot in diameter. Feeling back in there with his hand revealed space; lots of space with a rock ceiling!

He started removing dirt and small rocks, digging again with the hatchet. It would be really dull after today's workout thought Bran. By working another hour he had dug down and removed enough rocks so he could fit his body through. His flashlight, part of the ten essentials a hiker should carry, revealed only darkness. He knew he couldn't go down in there without help and the right equipment.

Of all the mines Bran had cataloged, none had made him feel like he had done more than a good day's work. The euphoria he felt now bordered on hysteria. He could hardly wait to tell Night.

Bran picked up his pack and from habit, looked around to see if he had left anything. He even set the fern back beside the hole. Not to cover it, but to give the fern a chance to live. He then traversed back up the trail and turned on the track that went over the cliff top. He came out on the other side of the meadow. No trouble at all!

Walking back towards the meadow, he looked around to see if he had missed the entrance to the cave. Careful exploration revealed nothing. By hanging onto the Douglas fir tree and leaning out, he could just barely make out the black mark the smoke from the chimney had made on the underside of the cliff.

It was getting late. He had to leave before it got too dark, since he didn't want to stay at the guard station tonight. He wanted to see Night.

As he left the meadow, two ravens settled in the Douglas fir tree. Bran looked back at their raucous call. He grinned and waved at them His Indian yell echoed through the hills as he loped down the trail.

CHAPTER *8*

PREPARE TO SPELUNK

Bran did double-time all the way back to the Ross Lake Guard Station. As he crossed over the majestic Ross Dam, he looked over to where the Guard Station was located. The lights weren't on nor was the boat tied up over there, that meant no one was there yet. He might as well take the trail up to the North Cross State Highway where his truck was parked.

Another half-hour and he was at the truck. It was a good thing too, he thought, as it was almost dark. If he wanted to see Knight before everyone went to bed, he needed to get going.

The drive back to the Ranger Station at Marblemount was long enough for Bran to realize he should give more thought to his discovery. He and Night were the only ones to even care about the preservation if there was an old mine up there. If he told the rest of the crew, there might be more people overrunning the meadow than need be. Or the cave could just be a hole in the ground and good old staid Bran Donovan would look like a fool. Better to tell Night what he had found and see if she got excited. No matter what, he needed to get spelunking equipment and let someone know where he could be located in an emergency.

At the Ranger Station, Bran parked the pickup in its stall, wrote the mileage down and locked it up, then with long strides, headed for the bunkhouse. He opened the door and stepped in, looking at the few people that were still up watching TV. There was no sign of the dark-haired girl he was looking for.

"Has anyone seen Night?" he asked the room at large. Noticing that all he got was some raised eyebrows, he remembered she had another name.

"Sorry about that, I meant Sunny."

One of the girls giggled. "Sure Mr. Donovan, Sunny went to read in her bunk. I'll go get her."

In a few seconds, Sunny and the other girl came back into the room. Sunny was in her terrycloth robe and slippers.

"Hi Bran, what's up?" inquired Sunny.

"I was going to ask you to come over to the motor home. I wanted to see if you could work with me tomorrow, but I see I'm too late tonight."

"If it's important Bran, I can get dressed and come over; however, tomorrow is my day off."

"Great! Give me fifteen minutes to clean up a little and I'll treat you to a cold 7-Up," and with that Bran left, quietly shutting the door behind him.

With the shutting of the door, Sunny was treated to teasing remarks by the crew. After all, if you didn't get teased, it meant the crew was too sick to care. Sunny took it all in stride and went back to her bunk area to change. She slipped into a black velour jumpsuit with leopard skin belt. This looked too dressed up for the occasion, but Sunny had found out this was very practical for just sitting around the TV area after showering. She slipped the matching headband onto her hair to hold it back and left via the TV room.

"Well, over to the slave driver's headquarters," Sunny

grumbled as she went out the door. Working on her day off? "Humph!" A few wolf whistles followed as the door closed.

Sunny knocked on the motor home door. No answer, but she could hear the shower running. She opened the door and went in. The sliding door to the back area was closed, so Bran must have expected her to come on in if he didn't answer.

About that minute, the shower went off, there was some banging and slamming around, then Bran emerged through the sliding door. His shirt was hanging out of his pants, but it was buttoned. His hair was wet and his feet were bare, but to Sunny he looked great. There was an excitement about him that was totally different from the taciturn man she was getting to know.

"Glad to see you're here Night, er—Sunny. We'll talk as soon as I nuke a TV dinner in the microwave." He took one from the freezer part of the refrigerator and putting it into the microwave, set the timer on it for the required minutes.

"Now, here's your 7-Up, or would you like something else to drink, a beer or orange juice?"

"No, a 7-Up is just fine. I love white wine, but the water up here over ice cubes is just about the best drink there is," smiled Sunny as she accepted the soda.

As Bran opened his beer, the microwave timer went off, so he took his dinner out. He put it down on the bar and straddled a stool.

"Go ahead, sit down, Night. I'll talk as I eat." He nodded at the seating area.

Sunny selected one of the white leather chairs. As she sat there waiting, Bran looked her over. God she's pretty, he thought.

"Well, Night, I went up to your meadow today."

This brought Sunny out of her chair and over to the bar. She had to hoist herself up to get on the barstool. Oh, the disadvantages of being short, she thought.

"And after spending the day exploring around," Bran took a bite of his food as he continued, "I think I've found a cave."

Sunny's eyes lit up at this information. "Do you really think there is something up there, Bran?"

"I sure do and I want you to go up there with me to explore this cave. You're not afraid of caves are you? I never gave that a thought. I just knew I wanted you to share whatever we found." Conflicting emotions raced over Bran's face.

"No, I'm not afraid to go into a cove, but I haven't done any of that before. Do I need to know anything special?" This worried Sunny a little, even in her excitement. She would hate to look stupid in front of him.

"No, you don't need to know anything special as I'll be with you. I know you already know how to rappel and climb back up, plus we'll rope together if things look bad, like rock fissures or drop-offs."

At that, Sunny's eyes opened wide, but never would she let on that this worried her.

"I take it this isn't a cave we just walk into with electric lights shining down the pathways?" Sunny smiled at her little joke trying to lighten her attitude towards the cave.

Bran laughed a harsh laugh. "No way. We have to go through a hole I found and dug out enough for my body to slip through. We'll have to rappel down about fifteen feet, I figure." He looked seriously at her before he continued, "From there I don't know where it will go. If it's a mine shaft, it will go back farther into the mountain or even down."

Mulling it over he continued, "I doubt if it will go very far down considering the water flowing from under the slide area. If it does, that part will be filled with water. What I could see with the flashlight was only rock and a dim floor area. Now! When can we go?"

Bran asked this last question like a little boy wanting to go to the zoo. His grin was totally unlike the fellow Sunny first met.

Sunny looked at this man and thought, I'll go anywhere with you big guy—to the moon—to the stars—or even into a cave.

However, she told him, "I have the next two days off. I'll donate them to you just for the fun of it. But! As you've been gone all day, you probably don't know that we're all on call for a lightning storm that has already caused some fires south of us over at Darrington. The lightning was hitting north around Mr. Baker last I heard. It may work its way east over here later this evening. If it causes any fires, you know we'll all have to stay in radio contact or stay close to the station."

Now that Night had mentioned it, Bran could hear thunder a distance away. He had been so excited he hadn't given the noise a thought. Damn! He so wanted to pursue this right now.

At Bran's disappointed look, Sunny's true nature came to the forefront. As a teacher, she had been trained to solve problems in everyday kindergarten life, so problems she would solve.

"Come on big guy, tell me your plan. We can get organized and if nothing comes of the storm, we can get permission to explore and take a radio with us to keep in contact with the Ranger Station."

At this, Bran brightened up. Now why didn't he think of that?

"Sure, then no one will be left holding a fire fighting Pulaski tool, without a warm body to swing it, if we don't get back in time for you to work your regular schedule."

"Gee, thanks! I can see you're just a real easy going boss, like working me twenty four hours a day, seven days a week!" Sunny grinned, not at all put out by this suggestion.

"Okay! To work girl," ordered Bran. He got another drink for both of them. "Let's share the work. Could you plan the food for two days? We'll take our tents, sleeping bags, water proof pads, a few candles, plus one canister propane stove should do for both of us, with an extra cylinder."

He marked some notes on a piece of paper. "I could eat everything out of my Sierra cup, but I do like instant coffee with my meal, so I have a tin plate in my pack. Gather the cooking pans you'll need. I'll get together all the spelunking gear. We'll share the load, but we'll keep your pack to about twenty-five pounds. Have you anything to add to this list?"

"Can I take my eyelash curler and my Teddy bear?" Sunny replied in a little girl's high voice.

Bran looked shaken for a moment. "Sorry Night. I'm not used to working with anyone and when I do, I give the orders. I know, you know all about backpacking. In fact, all you girls have done a good job this year. It seems the smaller they are, the harder they work. I've heard that from the big boss himself." Bran gave Sunny a smile meant to nullify his bossiness.

Unbeknown to Bran, that smile from him would have brought Sunny to her knees if she had been standing.

With the same smile on his face, he added, "I can be ready by ten tomorrow morning, but let's keep the cave our secret for now. We don't want the area over-run with people while we're investigating."

Sunny slid off her stool in a trance and headed for the door. Bran followed her. At the door, she turned and fluttered her eyelashes at him, then quietly said, "Make it nine!"

"Minx!" laughed Bran. "Did I tell you how beautiful you look tonight?" Staring into her eyes, he leaned down and lightly kissed the upturned lips.

Again Sunny floated back to the crew house. There would never be a beaten path from the motor home to the crew house. Sunny always floated back on wings of air.

The next morning right on schedule, Sunny was ready to go as Bran pulled up to the motor home in the pickup truck.

"You're ready I see," said Bran. "I forgot to tell you to bring your hardhat."

"I've got it, and some of fire fighting gear if needed. I've heard we didn't get any fires last night, but tonight might be another story," answered Sunny.

"Can you carry that larger axe and shovel along with all the food and pans you seem to have packed? I told you we would share the load," voiced Bran with concern.

"I'll be right as long as you keep us near water. All our food is dried. We can last a week with what I've packed. I've got a roll of tin foil for pans and one coffeepot to boil water in, plus a collapsible plastic jug to hold water. I've got lots of plastic bags for mixing and storing food. Why, except for the wine, we'll have a candle light dinner, my friend," reported Sunny.

"Where did you get it all? I expected to stop at the store. You just had to get the menus." This was said as Bran loaded the packs in the back of the truck and threw a tarp over them in case of a rain shower.

Sunny got in the truck on the other side as Bran hopped in and started backing out. "Well, I was supposed to leave on another back country trip after my days off, but the fire danger changed that. I'm using what my partner and I would have used if we had gone. I'll replace it when I get back."

Bran remembered. "That's right. I was able to get permission to use you for the extra two days only because of the fire danger. I've got a radio too, with orders to check in each morning and night. I've told everyone I'm checking out a mine area. I also signed in approximately where we'd be. No one blinked an eye at the area but I guess I'm supposed to be the expert on mines, so no one questioned me." Bran whipped the truck into one of the Marblemount stores. "Be back in a minute." Sure enough, he was only gone a short time. He stowed whatever he bought in his pack before he started the truck again, and headed towards the long drive up the Skagit River.

CHAPTER 9

THE CAVE

The ride was uneventful, filled with small talk. The hike was getting to be a familiar one, although this time they tried their ponchos to the top of their packs for use if it started to rain. The clouds were very low down on the lake. There wasn't a mountain showing. It could have been a lake with small rolling hills around it if seen for the first time. The hikers knew majestic peaks surrounded this mountain lake. Many were snow-capped or glaciated all year. Some thunder sounded far off in the distance.

The hikers hurried a little faster hoping the rain would hold off long enough to set up camp and do a little exploring. It did. They got to the meadow. Bran showed Sunny, the way up over the cliff, to the left of the meadow. They had to go by the pile of rocks that before had resembled a primitive outhouse. It looked more like one now that they were sure there was a cave up there and probably a mine of some kind.

"We could set up camp here if you'd like," said Bran, "or we could explore the cave and see if it's dry?"

Even though it was phrased as a sentence giving her the choice, Sunny could see Bran really wanted to explore.

"Oh, let's explore a little," said Sunny, knowing she had made the right choice when she got a knockout smile from Bran.

"You know Night, you're a girl after my own heart."

She followed him up over the cliff, thankful that he didn't know how right he was.

Even though Bran wanted to hurry, he shortened his stride and helped Sunny up several long steps. He took care going down the other side towards the creek. They came to the deer trail that followed along the ravine. Sunny stopped here and looked both ways.

"How far up the creek does this trail go?"

"Just to the area above the falls," said Bran pointing up the creek, then pointing the other way, "and just to that big rock in the path over by the slide area."

"It's strange, but it looks man made to me," said Sunny. "It's my job to look trails over. I'm not even sure what I know is wrong, but no deer made this path. They just used it."

"Come on. The cave is over beyond the big rock. There's just enough room for the two of us if we're careful."

They traversed to the rock and carefully went around it. Bran removed the fern he had placed in front of the hole.

Sunny looked at the opening Bran had dug out. "My god! Is that our cave? What do you think I am; some kind of mole?" Her expression was horrified.

Bran was more than surprised at her attitude. "Now Night girl, you've done just great so far. Let's keep up that bright sunny disposition for awhile longer. Here, take my flashlight and look in there before you get all stubborn on me.

"If you'll just let me get out of my pack first, I've got a flashlight of my own in my fisherman's vest. I've got four days to work up enough spunk to go down into that hole so don't rush me," pouted a slightly scared Sunny.

"Okay, okay," Bran said trying to pacify her. "I'm just excited.

Last time I was here it was all I could do to keep myself from going down there. Now that you're here, I can and it's all I can do to stop myself from just jumping in."

Bran was already unloading the climbing gear. "I'll go down first and check it out. Then I'll let you come down when you're ready. As you said, we have four days to explore this area."

While talking, Bran had already flipped the rope around the big rock and tied it off. He got into his climbing harness. The other harness was for Night if she wanted it. He tied another rope to his harness. He put his hardhat on, checked his flashlight and handed the other end of the rope to Sunny.

"Well, I'm ready. You can belay me down while I rappel with the rope I tied around the big rock."

Sunny looked stupidly at the rope he handed to her.

"I said, belay me down Night."

Sunny jumped, "You stupid ass. I'm so scared I'd probably drop you if I tried to belay right now."

"Oh Night girl, I'm sorry!" Bran put his arms around her. Sunny dropped her head against his chest.

"You're going down into that deep dark hole. What if something happened? At this moment I couldn't go in and help you."

"Yes, you would. I know you. You would fight the devil if you thought it was the right thing to do. As far as I can see, I'll only be going down about fifteen feet. Since I'm over six feet tall that leaves only nine feet for me to drop. Now, come on sweetheart and get behind that big rock to belay me down."

Sunny lifted her face to look at him, concern in her eyes. He lowered his head and kissed each eye, then her delectable mouth. Even if it's cussing him out, it's still delectable, he thought.

Sunny slowly pulled away and carefully got on the other side of the big rock.

"Belay on," she called, "let's get this show on the road," her bravado, sounding better than she felt.

Bran threw the tied-off rope down the opening. He had to go in backwards. He called for a little slack from the belay rope. Sunny gave him some as she felt the pull. She would have all his weight for a second while he slid through the hole.

"Belay on." Bran called.

Sunny felt the tug. He must be through.

"Slack!" he yelled.

She fed him down. No problem!

"Belay off," yelled Bran. "I'm down."

Sunny stayed on duty holding the belay rope. Bran flashed the light around. He was in a room. The floor was solid rock as was the ceiling, rounding in a curve to form the back wall. The wall where he had come down was rocked up. The cave went around the corner just out of sight. In the other direction, towards the slide area was: "My god!" said Bran, "it's a door! Night come over and peer down here."

Sunny left her rope and carefully went around the rock over to the cave entrance. She leaned down. "Well, what's down there?" she called?

"You'll never believe it but it's a nice room with a door. If you'll hand me down the axe tied on the other rope, I'll test the timbers to see if there is any dry rot. It looks like good dry cedar."

Sunny got the axe and tied it to the belay rope. "Heads!" she called and then lowered the axe.

Bran took the axe and went over to the door. He gently tapped around the casings. The whole wall area had been neatly tongue and grooved in the old dovetail style. If it were free from dry rot, it would be as strong as the rock around it. He tried the door. It was stuck shut.

"You can come down now, Night, if you want to. It's a neat cave."

"How can I come down? Who'll belay me?"

"I could catch you if you fall, but throw the belay rope around the rock and the other end to me, then I'll belay you down. I could sure use the candles also."

"How about me sending my pack down then if we get stuck, I'll have food—you can starve?"

"Okay, but we'll need water or your food will sure taste awful."

"Bully! I'll send the candles." Sunny dug in one of the pockets of her pack and produced a sack of candles.

"Here! Catch!"

Bran caught the sack and took one candle out then lit it with matches from his pocket. Looking around for a place to put it, he noticed a niche beside the door. Going over there, he looked in the hole. There was a candleholder made out of tin with a reflector in the back. The mice had long ago eaten the candle out. He put his candle in it and again looked for a place to set the candleholder. Yes, there was a ledge just at the bend of the cave. He set the holder there. Made for it, he thought.

"Okay, Bully! I'm ready when you are," cried a voice from the opening.

"You can't be until I untie my harness," replied Bran.

In a few short minutes small boots came through the opening. "My you've got a cute butt," chuckled, Bran, and got dirt in his face for looking up.

Sunny scrambled down, rappelling against the rock. Her fears vanished as she looked around the room. It wasn't large, but it was dry and cool. She untied from the rope.

"Shall we look around?" she quipped.

"I thought you'd never ask," laughed Bran delightedly. His girl was made of the right stuff. Jolted, when had he begun to think of her as 'his girl'?

Bran got the candle and they turned to go to the back of the cave, tunnel or whatever. Just around the bend, out of sight of the candlelight when it was on the ledge, was the end of the cave. But what an end! Both persons stopped and stared. Sunny grabbed Bran's arm.

"What is it?" she stared at very old bones on the floor.

He stared at rows and rows of canned food in very old blue jars. They were setting on hand hewed cedar planks made into shelves. A few jars had been knocked over and broken. Dust and cobwebs were on everything.

Two bats startled by the light flew around before going out the hole. Sunny screamed a little, but only because she was startled. She still stared at the bones.

Bran looked at them and then at her.

"I think they are just animal bones. Looks like maybe a deer." The bones were almost powdered. In fact, some parts looked just like dried dirt. It was hard to tell. A cougar might have dragged a deer in here, but he wasn't about to mention that to Night.

Some old horse harness hung back there on a peg, badly chewed. A collection of tools was there in very good condition. They had been treated with a type of grease, hand rubbed into them. They looked sturdy but the handles would probably break if touched. All this stuff was a collector's dream. A lantern hung from a wire over a workbench. Everything was layered in dust, plus with scat sign he knew a few animals had lived here, as did the marmot Bran had seen that first day.

Again, Sunny was the first to spot the shattered remains of a cup and saucer. They were lying on the floor next to the workbench. A large flat rock was on the floor.

If the cup and saucer had fallen anywhere else it might have landed in the dirt, but the rock had shattered the delicate pottery.

"Well, here's the answer to the pottery mystery," Sunny said as she picked up a large piece of the cup. "Animals must have carried pieces out of here and then the ravens stole the pieces away from them."

"You're probably right. Now, if we just knew why all this was down here hidden away. I need to get through the door to see what that chimney is all about," said Bran looking thoughtful.

"What chimney? You didn't tell me about a chimney."

"I'm sorry Night. I was so anxious to get down here I forgot to show you the chimney. Let's go back to the door and see if I can budge it."

They started back to the cave entrance. It was just a few short steps around the bend.

"Oh! Oh! It's raining. We need to get our packs down here or get out and set up our camp. It's your choice, Night. Bran looked down at her.

Sunny eyed the opening apprehensively. "I'm not sure I can stay down here without the light, Bran."

"Let's blow it out and see. Get your flashlight ready so you can turn it on quickly."

Sunny reached into her front pocket on the vest. "Okay, I'm ready."

Bran blew out the candle. The light from the entrance wasn't much but after a few seconds of getting used to the dark, Sunny's eyes became accustomed to the lesser light and she could see quite well.

"I think I can handle this if you will knock down a few more cobwebs in this area by the door. It doesn't have the bones here anyway."

Bran smiled at her. His voice reverberated against the wall. "It sure beats getting our butts wet out there. Come on cave girl, let's get out of here, get some water and then make a cozy camp down here. It's starting to get late anyway."

Bran helped Sunny out first. They scrambled into their ponchos. "I'll go fetch the water, Night, if you'll get me the container, plus, if you give me your axe I've got an idea on how to make a ladder."

At her look, he smiled sheepishly. "I know I'm not supposed to deface the trees, but I promise to take just a few limbs out of sight."

"That's what they all say," she grumbled, but handed him her axe. "While you're gone, I'll lower our packs. I've got a rope that goes with my tent, which I can use."

With a nod, Bran took off. Sunny got her rope out. It was wrapped in a tarp she would have put over her tent to help deflect the rain. It was raining harder now. Pretty soon water would be dripping into the cave from the opening Bran made enlarging the entrance. In fact, it was getting muddy where she stood.

Sunny took her tarp and stretched it over the entrance. She secured it with large boulders from the slide area. One end of the tarp went over the big boulder and another on the other side in the slide area. Stretching the tarp she glanced up and saw the smoke-area on the rock face and leaned over to look down the chimney. She had to scramble out onto the rocks to do so. Bran, being taller probably had just leaned out over it.

Very interesting, she thought. Just what was on the other side of the cave door, besides the rock slide area? Looking her tarp over, she wished she could get under it. She had an idea. Around the big rock she went. A short distance away, she found a long, branch from one of the trees, its needles long gone. She dragged it back to the cave entrance.

There she propped it up under the tarp against the face of the rock cliff. She again started piling rocks on the tarp near the slide. This made the area under the tarp higher. Next a few rocks held the end down. A few slid over the ravine edge, but there were lots more rocks where those came from.

As busy as a little marmot making a nest, she then secured the pole with a few more rocks. She had to reposition the rock on the big boulder next to the cave hole and viola! a tent. Only about four feet high but it was dry. The tent even had an entrance where it was propped up by the big boulder.

With extra rope, she then lowered Bran's pack into the cave. My god! It was heavy. But bracing her feet, she lowered it. For her pack, she pulled the rappel rope back out. It was long. She lowered her pack with that.

With the radio she had removed from Bran's pack, she did their check in and signed off. With the rain, there shouldn't be any fire problems.

She heard a whistling tune and realized Bran would be there soon. The man must have rocks in his head to be whistling in this downpour.

"Hey, Night, I'm coming. Well, well, what have we here? You've decided to camp on this five-foot ledge. A little short for a six footer, don't you think?" A dripping head appeared under the tarp. A hand with the water carrier came next held out like an offering.

"I have to get my sticks and the axe, then my girl, we'll have a nice cozy, little tying contest." More sticks appeared and then the axe.

Sunny quickly stacked things out of the way of the big hulk that would soon have to get under the tarp, also.

"That's it. Here I come." For a big person, Bran was very careful when he entered the tent. "Miss me?" he grinned and kissed her upturned face. He couldn't see in the dull light, but Sunny knew she was blushing. Even wet, he's a hunk!

He tied off the belay rope around the rock, then quickly started fashioning a ladder between the belay and rappel ropes. "Some of the steps will probably be at a crooked slant, but it will hold the ropes apart.

They talked about their find as they sat there tying the rope ladder. Sunny helping where she could, Bran finally finished the ladder to his satisfaction.

"We're ready. Do you want to go first?"

"No way! You go down and brush the cobwebs away. Light the candle and generally get ready for the queen of the house. My job will be to make the mud pies and sprinkle dandelion blossoms on the top!" Sunny grinned, referring to childhood days when everything was '*Let's pretend*'. Bran was halfway in the cave. He grinned back at her, "My sister never let me be the daddy. I was always the little kid or the dog." He grabbed the water jug and disappeared. She heard cursing. Pretty soon, "All clear," was sounded.

Sunny picked up the radio and proceeded to scramble down the precarious ladder.

"Watch your knuckles," Bran called. "I scraped mine as I came down."

He had removed the packs so she wouldn't stumble over them. Then got out the small stove, spread its legs apart, attached the gas cylinder, then took a match and lit it.

Smiling Bran said, "Thou fire awaits you, my Queen."

"Why thank you kind sir." Sunny smiled back at him.

Sunny busied herself with getting together a supper. She had planned to make pans from tin foil and a stick, but had forgotten to bring down the right stick. So, 'Plan 2', instant chicken noodle soup in the Sierra cups, cheese and sailor crackers, instant chocolate pudding mixed in a plastic sack and served in tin foil bowls, then instant coffee using the extra Sierra cups she had stuck in, mindful of Bran wanting coffee with his meal. She did the work quickly, mixing the pudding as the water heated.

She got out her waterproof sleeping pad and spread it against the rock wall. Her part was done. Dinner was ready.

Meanwhile, Bran was looking the door area over and exploring the cave area again. The small amount of heat from the propane stove was warming the cave. It felt good. Bran looked at Night, sitting cross-legged on her pad, ready to serve dinner.

"Ah, my candlelight dinner awaits and I have just the thing to go with it." Bran announced going to his pack. He rummaged around in it and brought out a bottle of white wine and a small pack of plastic see-through glasses.

"You carried that up here, and I didn't break it when I lowered your pack down here?" exclaimed an astonished Sunny.

"Yeah, well, I forgot about it until just now." He uncorked the bottle and poured them each a plastic glass full. He would never make a wine steward with those glasses, but emoted a refinement at odds with the cave they were in. Sunny was impressed. He had remembered she liked white wine. As they ate, they discussed tomorrow's strategy.

CHAPTER *10*

THE SURPRISE

The next morning they decided to pry the door open. In the back of the cave, Bran had found a crowbar, pick, and nearly every tool he needed to do the job. After trying them he found their hickory handles as good as the day they were made.

After breakfast of instant oatmeal, instant orange drink, and lots of coffee, they rolled their sleeping bags and moved everything to the storage area in case something collapsed around the door.

Bran said, "It might be wise for you to go topside with the radio in case something happens. You could do our morning check-in while you're up there, too."

Sunny climbed the shaky ladder. After she called in, she decided to explore while Bran worked on the door. Even in the rain, it felt good to be out in the fresh air. She walked back to the falls. Knowing trails, she was convinced this was man made. It remained only because the deer had kept it from going back to nature.

At the falls, looking around the ravine she could guess where the big boulder had come from. It diverted some of the water to this side, to cascade in pools down the cliff. Pockmarks in the steep side hill above showed signs of the old slides. Avalanches of snow or rock seemed to be common to this area as evidence shown in the slide on the face of the rock cliff in front near the meadow.

Since the trail ended here, she explored more of the area. She leaned over and looked down the top of the falls where all the little pools were. It actually looked like log cribbing down there. Only humans could have stacked logs one upon another like that. Water disappeared in swirls into the logs.

This mystery made her slowly follow the trail back to the cave, looking over the side every so often. In one area that had eroded the trail from underneath, she got down and really looked. By brushing away some of the moss, she actually thought she had found a large pipe.

Finding a stick she dug around the eroded area some more. Sure enough, pipe about eight inches in diameter was running under the trail straight to the cave area, if she should venture a guess. Excited she rushed the rest of the short distance to the cave entrance.

Under the tarp Bran sat pensively. Sunny excitedly told him what she had found. Bran, looking neither surprised nor excited, just stated "That figures."

Sunny, looking a little hurt, replied "What's wrong? I thought you of all people would really be excited."

"Well, I'll tell you. I finally opened the door and you can scrap any mine theory. Come on down. It's a shrine of some kind, but it doesn't look dangerous. In fact, it smells of old cedar; like opening your grandmother's trunk. I didn't look around much except to see if it was safe. I wanted to share it with you."

"That was sweet of you." Sunny was touched by his thoughtfulness.

Bran could feel the warmth of his ears turning red. He

had never considered himself sweet. He didn't tell her either that as he had opened the door and the cedar smell had hit him, blackness had come at him in waves. The raven in his mind flew at him again. He'd had to sit down, thinking the air was too thin for him in the cave. After his heart had slowed down a little, he had gone in.

Now, as he approached the door with Night, nothing happened. He had almost expected the raven to fly at him again. Bran stooped to get through the short door and both of them stepped over the threshold. Straightening up, he held the candle high so she could get a better look.

Sunny was astounded. Here was the nicest little cabin she had ever seen. It was not very big by today's standards, but it had everything it needed to be comfortable. The air wasn't too good in here yet, but the candle was staying lit.

"I'll get more candles," Sunny said as she spotted a couple of candleholders with the no candles in them.

Sunny came back in with four candles and placed one near the stove on the wall where a candleholder was held in place by a wooden peg. She took two others and placed them in candleholders on the table. The previous candles had long ago been eaten by the mice. Just remnants remained scattered around on the table. She took her last candle and placed it in a holder on the small nightstand near the bed. As she placed the candles, Bran lit them from his candle. To their eyes that had already adjusted to the dark room, the resulting light in the room was as illuminating as any hundred-watt electric light bulb.

The soft glow highlighted the objects in the room making a charming, old-fashioned cabin. Sunny and Bran stood there in awe. It was unbelievable. Everything had been preserved like the person had just left it not long ago. The air was very stuffy.

There was a light sprinkling of dust over everything. They could see the mice had left sign, but for the most part the room was preserved as if waiting for the return of the owner.

The huge built-in bed beside them was covered with a handmade quilt. It had been pieced together in random pieces of material that Sunny recognized as the '*Crazy Quilt*' pattern. This style of quilt was made to utilize every scrap of material. Sunny, giving the bed a couple of deep pats, heard the mattress crinkle and realized it must be stuffed with straw. People used to do that, and change the straw when it got matted down. She had read that it was like changing the sheets. At that time the smell of the straw was as delightful as the fresh-air smell of sheets that had been hung outside to dry.

Her patting raised a little dust. "This bed looks comfortable but needs a little shaking to get the dust out of the quilt."

"Yeah! Better than our water proof pads we slept on last night," Bran added, doing his couple of pats, also. "There were a couple of rocks I just couldn't get away from."

"But it was dry," chuckled Sunny raising her eyebrows and looking sideways at him. As they exchanged small talk, their eyes were taking in the rest of the room. The table had been set for two as if expecting to eat at any minute. A beautiful hutch to the left of them, placed against the rock wall, held as assortment of dishes. Sunny reminded herself to check these out later.

On the rocked up end wall, a teakettle sat on the old fashioned wood stove, along with a large cast iron Dutch Oven. Beside the stove was a Kitchen Queen, used as a cupboard and baking center in the olden days. Next in line was the sink area with an old hand pump protruding from the small counter and hanging over the sink. Above the sink a mirror with a shelf imbedded in the rock wall under it held a shaving mug and a comb. A bucket, with a dipper hanging on a nail above it, sat on the other side of the sink in the corner.

Next was the door to the outside that would probably go to the meadow if it could be opened. A few wooden pegs had been drilled into the log wall by the door to hold hats or coats. On this same wall, a set of three windows had a small table with a beautiful oil lamp placed there for light for the two rocking chairs flanking it. The windows looked like they had been boarded up from the outside or possibly had shutters.

A closet hugged the corner. The bed was against the same wall, filling the rest of it. A footlocker or trunk was at the foot of the bed.

"A very cozy cabin," exclaimed Sunny, nodding her head and pursing her lips in contemplation.

The sight of the pump was too much for Bran. He went over to it and started working the handle. Like a little boy in a toy store, the stove beckoned him next. He raised one of the lids and looked inside, clanking around some more.

Sunny ignored Bran's playing with the pump and stove. She cautiously opened the closet next to the bed. In the closet, there wasn't room for many clothes, but the few there, were a collector's delight. Very carefully she touched them for fear they might dissolve into dust at her feet. She removed a dress. It was rather a large dress and long, and looked like the style found in the eighteen hundreds. Its rich brown color, high neck, long sleeves and velvet trim against the wool, would have made it a very serviceable dress rather than stylish.

"Bran, look at this dress. Where do you think this could have come from?"

Bran looked up from where he was at the pump again. "Uh, I don't know," he replied, obviously not interested in a dress when a good old fashioned pump was at hand.

Sunny carefully placed the dress back in the closet. She was afraid of disturbing the contents too much since their obvious age would make them fragile. Fragile they may be, but they were in awfully good condition. She slowly took out a man's suit. Even though the styles haven't changed much over the years, this style went back a long way.

It was the type of suit you bought as a young man, wore all your life and was buried in. She carefully put the suit back. Up above on the self, she spied a bowler hat. This was just too much of a temptation. Taking it down, she put it on her head and started the old '*Charlie Chaplin*' walk.

"Hey Bran! How do I look now?"

"Very funny! But do you think we should be fooling around with their personal stuff? We don't know what we've stumbled on." Bran grinned to take the sting out of his reprimand.

"You're right. Oh! Don't touch anything more, Bran. I've got to get my camera to take pictures of this. In the excitement of getting in here I totally forgot to record what we've found."

It was part of Sunny's duty to take pictures of hazardous areas or damage done by nature or backpackers. At all times her camera was with her. She quickly went back through the door to the area where her backpack was.

Coming back in the room, she systematically took pictures of the individual area in the room. A few flashes and they both were seeing bubbles in the air. She got Bran's picture standing by the pump.

"Will you open the hutch, Bran? I'd like to get a picture of those dishes in there also."

Bran went around the table to this beautiful antique. The workmanship on this piece was excellent. The leaded glass, in the doors, was of clear cut glass, which let you see through to the Blue Delft dishes artistically arranged behind them. Bran dutifully opened the doors so Sunny could do her job.

"Could you take a close-up of the pump for me, Night? That pump is a real old-timer."

Sunny focused on a close-up of the pump, then the Kitchen Queen and last, in line the stove. Her immediate job finished, Sunny noticed a dishtowel hiding something on the Kitchen Queen. Opening it up it looked like the remains of a loaf of bread. Mice had eaten some of it, plus a few bites of the dishtowel too. It was as hard as a rock.

Next, Sunny looked in the old black Dutch Oven. Something had been in it, but now all that was there was a dried up black lump. Nothing was in the stove's oven. The old stove had a few rust spots on its top and certainly was dusty, but otherwise it was in very good shape. Bran was still squeaking the pump handle. The noise was very grating in the closed atmosphere of the room.

"I'm going to get some of our water and see if I can prime this pump. Everything seems to be in good condition, so it shouldn't hurt to try. I doubt if it will work but nothing ventured, nothing gained."

Bran stepped through the small door, retrieved the plastic jug of water and ducked back through. He poured water down the pump, pumping the handle up and down as the water gurgled down the pipe. There was a slight suction noise but nothing happened.

"Bran, will you pour some of that water in the wash pan hanging there on the wall. I can't stand seeing the dust in here."

Bran handed her a pan of water and a rag he found hanging there also. She set the pan on one of the benches that matched the table. Quickly, she started wiping the whole place down.

While Sunny cleaned, Bran had lost interest in the pump and started checking out the wood stove. Moving a lever, he shook the old ashes down. On checking the chimney, he noticed a damper. Turning it a few times produced a few clunking sounds, but otherwise everything seemed to be all right.

"Night, I think I'll try starting a fire in the stove. It would warm us up a little and take the dampness out of the air."

Apprehensively, Sunny looked at him. "If you get that thing going and it starts to smoke we won't be able to stand it in here."

"I thought I'd start with a few twigs to see where the smoke goes before getting carried away with a real fire. I'll check the upper part of the chimney before I do." So saying, Bran went out the door, ducking again.

CHAPTER *11*

PLAYING HOUSE

Meanwhile, Sunny's water was dirty from all her cleaning. Going towards the sink to empty her container, she stepped around a pile of debris on the floor. On closer inspection, she realized it was a very dirty, stained old quilt. Dark stains had soaked into the cedar-planking floor. It looked like someone had been using the quilt to clean up the mess, and left in the middle of it. Sunny picked up her camera and took a close-up picture of this area.

Then, her *'little woman'* instincts came forward again. Trying not to get herself dirty, she carefully rolled the old quilt up. Not knowing what to do with it, she took it over and placed it next to the wood-box. Removing the quilt had uncovered a chunk of wood, which she picked up and put in the wood-box.

This was very strange, she thought to herself. The rest of the cabin is in such good order, why is this mess on the floor? What happened here? She could hear Bran outside running something up and down the chimney. She turned back to the room. Even that little bit of dusting had made the room look lived in. If she could shake out the quilt on the bed, the place wouldn't even smell dusty.

At that moment Bran came back through the door, ducking again. "I don't know who made this door, but he must have been a dwarf. I have to duck every time I come in here."

With a lilt to her voice, "That's right Bran. Bitch, bitch, bitch, this place was made for little people like me. I can go in and out without blinking and eye."

"I know short stuff! This place really does look like you." He looked around in appreciation, "Miniature little door, miniature little cabin, why it's absolutely beautiful."

"Why Bran are you calling me beautiful? Are you—are you really giving me a compliment?" stuttered a surprised Sunny. This was something she was going to have to think about. He thought she was beautiful?

Bran again was kind of taken back. Sure, he thought she's beautiful, but he really wasn't about to tell her that just yet. However, giving her a big smile, he said, "Well Night! If the shoe fits, wear it."

Uncomfortable with the exchange they had just had he turned back to the stove, and poked around inside it. "I think I will put a few sticks in and see what happens."

Bran broke up some kindling taken from the wood-box. It was very dry and brittle. Carefully putting a few splinters in the back of the fire pit, he lit them with one of his waterproof matches. They caught fire even without paper for a starter. He put in some more slivers and closed the lid of the stove. He could hear the tinder snapping and popping.

A little smoke escaped from around the lids but then dissipated, presumably all the rest of the smoke went up the chimney. He opened the front of the stove where you normally would stoked the fire and shoved in a few of the larger chunks of wood. He checked to make sure the door to the cave was open. He wouldn't want to carbon monoxide them or use up all the oxygen.

Turning back towards Sunny, proud of his accomplishment, he asked, "Unless you feel like hiking out of here soon, Night, we could make this place real cozy for tonight and start back tomorrow. That would still give you a day to get ready for your next back county hike."

Looking at Bran's wistful face made her realize she could never willingly go against this man's wishes. Besides, there was just too much yet to explore and too many unanswered questions about this place.

If they went out now, the next time they came back the place would be overrun with Park Rangers and lord knows whom else. Never, would they get to finish the job they came to do, even if it wasn't a mine they had found.

"I think you're right, Bran. But I'm going to take time out before dark for a quick bath back at the falls, rain or no rain. No washing up yesterday, no washing up today. Sweating, perspiring, this place is going to smell worse than just dusty. It's going to stink."

A hearty laugh escaped Bran. "You're right Night. I could use a little of that water too."

Bran went over to the water jug and dumped the remaining water in the teakettle on the stove. There was a side reservoir in the stove. Bran opened the lid and looked in.

Except for some rust, it looked usable. He grabbed the bucket and the jug, then ducked back through the door.

Peeking back, he asked, "Do you think you could steady these as I lower them, when I get back?"

"Sure, I think so. If not we'll think of something, we've been very resourceful so far," smiled Sunny. "Do you need any help?"

"No. You go ahead and explore. You might even want to inventory some of this stuff. I'll be back soon. I'll call the Ranger Station to check in while I'm out there."

Sunny looked around. The candles were not going to last very long. She decided to blow out the two on the table. With the kerosene lantern hanging on a wire from the rafter near

the stove and the beautiful lamp on the small table near the
windows, there just might be some fuel in the cave. She thought
she remembered seeing some jugs back there. Everything else
was in pretty good shape, why not some lamp oil? She would
ask Bran about that when he got back. He would know where
to look since he had been poking around back there quite a
bit.

Meanwhile, Sunny went over to the sink. She thought; now
what was Bran doing to this pump? He poured water down
the top and pumped the handle. She took the teakettle and
carefully poured water down the top of the pump and pumped
the handle.

While she was pumping the handle, she could feel it starting
to pull harder. A few more pumps on the handle and dirty,
rusty water came spewing out.

"Ugh!" But she kept pumping, hoping the drain to the
sink was going someplace besides down under the sink into a
bucket. Her arms were getting tired but she kept pumping.
The water slowly cleared. She swished the dirt out of the sink
with her free hand. Not knowing what to do next, she took an
empty jar setting on the counter next to the sink and filled it
with water along with the teakettle. At least there would be
more water to prime the pump again. She could hardly wait
for Bran to get back so she could show him the water. It was
clean and smelled wonderful.

With the problem of water solved and Bran bringing more,
she looked around for some pans. She knew what they would
have for dinner. She had dried beef stew that only needed to
have water added and boiled. She had planned to serve biscuits
cooked by wrapping them around a stick and roasting them
over a campfire. You then poured honey down the hole left by
the stick. With the stove going, she might be able to make real
biscuits.

Opening the warming oven, she found all the pans she
would need. The pans were the old blue enamel ones like you
could still find down in Mexico. There were some chips out of

the enamel but nothing that would hurt the cooking. Cast iron frying pans were hanging from nails to the left of the stove. One of those would do just fine for baking the biscuits.

She opened the front of the stove. It needed more wood. She shoved more wood in and closed the door again. It started to crackle right away. She put the teakettle back on to heat water. Might as well not waste the wood, were her thoughts.

There was a noise back in the cave. Bran must be back.

"Hey Night! Could you come here and help me?"

Sunny went back into the cave. There was Bran's head sticking through the hole.

"Bran, I hate to tell you this but you had a long walk in the rain for nothing. I got the pump working while you were gone. The water looks good enough to use."

"You did what? How did you do that?" Bran said grinning. He was halfway through the hole and handing down the bucket, then the jug to Sunny. He soon followed maneuvering down the make shift ladder.

Sunny explained, "I did just like you did and poured some water down the pump and it worked this time."

Bran looked thoughtful. "It must have had time to swell the gaskets and make a seal to suck the water up."

"Oh! You beast! You could have told me it was my delicate hand that did it," pouted a smug looking Sunny.

Now that Bran was here, it reminded her of the candles. "Do you suppose there might be any kerosene or oil for the lamps back there?" She gestured towards the back of the cave. "The candles aren't going to last too long."

"I'll go look. I remember seeing some glass gallon jugs back there. I noticed because the jugs had carved wooden plugs in their tops."

Sunny followed Bran back to the work bench area. Under the bench were quite a few jugs filled with liquid. Taking one out Bran worked the plug out.

"Yes! It smells like something that would burn."

They took the jug back with them. Bran took down the

lantern, while Sunny fetched the beautiful lamp from the table by the windows. Taking a funnel, that Sunny hadn't seen him bring in, Bran filled the lantern and the lamp

"I sure hope this stuff is lamp oil. I'd hate to blow us to 'Kingdom Come', and no one would find us either."

"Oh god Bran shut up! It's spooky enough without that little thought."

Bran laughed again. He couldn't remember when he had laughed so much. Once in awhile a smile would happen, but a laugh, never in years. This little girl, no; woman, was good for him. What made her different? Bran took out his matches to light the lamps while he contemplated that thought

"Just a minute, Bran, I'll wait around the corner. If it blows I'll go tell everyone where to find you."

"You just do that little girl. I think I know what I'm doing. I wouldn't want you to watch and see how I do it either. Next thing I know, I'll find myself out of another job and you having all the fun of lighting the lamps."

While Sunny went about fixing the meal, Bran looked the big bed over. It was made up with a quilt on it. As it was dusty, he decided to go out and get his tarp. Like Sunny, his tarp would have gone over his tent if they had used it. Going back in the storeroom, he rummaged around in his pack for a minute, then decided to bring the pack back with him.

Coming through the small door his pack caught on the casing, pulling him off balance. He hit his head on the top of the door, and finally made it into the room, cursing all doors not made to regulation height.

Sunny laughed at him. "I think the door is kind of cute."

"You mountain gnomes would," Bran retaliated, rubbing his forehead.

Undaunted by anything as small as a cracked skull, Bran took his tarp out and flipped it over the quilt on the bed. Next, his down sleeping bag was shaken out and spread on top of the tarp. Patting the bed a few times, he swung his long legs onto it.

Spying an old guitar he picked it up and looked it over. The dust had dulled its finish some. He tried the strings gently. They made a soft twang. Feeling the strings were too delicate to really play, he set it back where he had found it.

Snuggling down with his hands behind his head, he remarked to Sunny, "This is not bad, a little noisy, but not bad at all," as he bounced a little on the flat surface. The straw ticking crackled, probably turning to dust under him, he thought.

"Just like a man, lie down and take a nap while the little woman cooks his supper."

"Now Night, I got the fire going. I'm even making the bed up for sleeping," Bran grinned from his relaxed spot on the bed.

"Well, I just hope you're making another one up on the floor. That's a big bed but it's not big enough for the two of us. Remember? No fraternizing among the employees."

Stating her ultimatum, Sunny continued her homemaking, humming an out-of-tune unidentifiable song as she rinsed and dried the dishes that had been left on the table. Then she carefully reset the table. The candles would make it very romantic. In her musing where had that thought come from, she wondered?

Bran lay there thinking. My God! I was imagining Night right here next to me before reminding me we need to keep our distances. He remembered last night as they had slept back in the cave, in their separate sleeping bags, with about three feet between them. Sometime during the night their bags had slowly slid to the center. By morning, the first thing he noticed was a cloud of black hair just below his face. A small mound of warm body, in a sleeping bag, was cuddled up against him. He had lain there thinking how nice that had felt.

In his wilder days, 'Before Nam', he had never really slept with a woman. Just *'Love'em and Leave'em'* was the practice the good old boys had preached. Now, his mind was thinking *'Love Her, and Never Let Her Go.'* With that pleasant song running through his mind, he slowly drifted off to sleep, just as Sunny had predicted he would.

The cabin was cozy warm even with the door to the storeroom open. Sunny finished making the stew. The fresh biscuits were in the warming oven over the stove. Looking at the sleeping Bran, reminded her of waking this morning, all cuddled up to Bran. She had looked up straight into his black sexy eyes. Both had looked startled for a second and had turned away from each other like the commercials on TV for bad breath. This thought brought a smile to Sunny's face.

CHAPTER 12

BRAN'S RAVEN

She decided to take Bran a cup of coffee before she served their meal. Fixing the instant coffee in one of the Delft cups, she took it over and set it on the nightstand near the bed. She then leaned over the sleeping Bran and gently shook his shoulder. As she leaned over him, her long black hair swung out on either side of her face. Bran, slowly waking, saw the raven wings coming at him with Night's face for its head. He was visibly startled, a horrified expression on his face.

"What is it, Bran?" exclaimed a suddenly frightened Sunny.

"Do that again. Lean forward with your hair swinging," demanded Bran.

Taken back, Sunny complied with his strange request.

"Again," Sunny leaned over him twice; three times; her hair swinging out. Each time her hair swung out it resembled black wings, just like the raven in his nightmares. Bran suddenly grabbed Sunny and pulled her to him, kissing her mouth in a hard kiss.

Sunny knocked off her feet, sprawled across him. "Will you tell me what this is all about? I try to be nice to you by bringing you a cup of coffee which seemed to terrify you and THEN I'm wrestled to the bed." Sunny's scowling face was not amused.

Bran gave her a brilliant smile. "You wonderful girl, you've just rid me of a nightmare, no psychologist or years of therapy, ever has. Now, whenever I see the Raven it will have your lovely face in it."

This man had really lost his marbles.

"What are you talking about?" said Sunny as she climbed over Bran to sit on the bed. Crossing her knees, Indian fashion, her hands resting on her legs, she demanded, "Tell me!"

Bran struggled to sit up, his back to the wall. He reached over for the coffee and hoped it was strong. "Okay, I'll tell you. It's a long story so come up here by me and make yourself comfortable while I tell it."

Sunny wiggled up beside Bran and leaned over to take his cup to share a swallow of his coffee. Sitting back relaxed, Bran told her the story of his Raven.

He told her of its first coming at him at times of waking from some trauma in Vietnam, then at home in the hospital. He had seen it with his eyes wide open when they found that second piece of pottery out in the meadow. The last time, was when he had opened the door to this cabin and nearly passed out.

He told her of the folklore of the Raven that had been passed down to him through his Indian relatives. Last, but not least, was his name. It was Irish, but his mother had picked it because it meant Raven. It had satisfied both the Irish and Indian heritage.

"I've spent my whole life so steeped in folklore from both Irish and Indian, that I wouldn't be surprised if I turned into a raven and flew out that hole in the cave to get out of here. I may never be rid of the Raven, Night, but now at least it will have your lovely face superimposed for the head. That shouldn't be too scary." Bran gave her a smug look as he said that last part.

Sunny was amazed by this tale. Here was a highly intelligent man, but with fears she could hardly imagine. Turning slightly to look him in the eye she said, "My god Bran you are a walking phobia. You're afraid to let anyone see your body. You're afraid of birds. You're a basket case!"

Bran's euphoria died right before her eyes. "That's right Night. I am a basket case; that's why I've stayed to myself most of the time. It's just since I met you that all these phobias have come to a head. But, believe-it-or-not, I think you're good for me. You're the only person I've told all my secrets to. Not even the hospital personnel knows all I've told you." Bran's usual serious face was back in place.

She could see the remote person he had been starting to surface again. To lose the teasing Bran, even with all his phobias, would break her heart. The compassion that was always part of Sunny's nature came forth.

"Oh love. Come here and let me hold you for a minute," said Sunny, who had said this same thing to a number of her kindergarten students. With their arms around each other, they slowly rocked back and forth.

After a short time of comforting Bran, Sunny backed off a little. "I love holding you Bran, but our supper is probably ruined by now."

A slightly embarrassed, Bran, who had started to enjoy this cuddling, realized it was time to get back on track again. "You're right, let's get to eating your meal before it's ruined. It smells delicious."

They crinkled and scrunched back off the big bed. "Well, well! Biscuits too, and they look as good as they smell, all high and fluffy. You can't beat a wood stove for making biscuits. I remember some jam in the back room. Let me get a jar. It will make those biscuits taste like manna from heaven." Bran left the room on his errand.

Sunny dug the rest of the wine out of Bran's pack. In the hutch she found a couple of wineglasses. They looked like crystal but it didn't matter. She would be very careful with them.

Wiping them clean she poured the wine into the glasses. As Bran came back in, what he saw would gladden the heart of any man.

The candles on the table reflected a warm glow off Sunny's face making it more beautiful than he had ever seen it. The glasses sparkled and the wine sent up tiny diamonds as it was poured from the bottle. If she had been in a long dress, it could have been a scene from '*Little House On The Prairie*', a Laura Ingalls Wilder book made into a TV show.

He looked quickly away, almost embarrassed by his observation. The jar had a snap closure on it. The rubber ring fell apart as he removed the glass lid, a truly antique jar. There was a wax seal that he carefully removed. This was very old jam and it smelled as fresh as the day it was made. Bran wiped the jar off and brought it to the table.

"Everything looks great," he told the beautiful lady.

Sunny beamed. She liked the compliment, but everything did look nice and to think this was a back packer's meal. Served on the Delft dishes made it special, plus the handsome man she was coming to know. Candlelight was magic for the room, the meal, and the people eating there. As they munched the biscuit the jam turned out to be blueberry.

"Tell me how you know how to cook on a wood stove?" asked Bran.

"My folks have one at the commune. It isn't used as much now, but that's what I learned to cook on first. The electricity came later. Our kitchen is a mixture of old and new. I relate to some of this stuff in here, even if I really wouldn't want to go back to the old ways again."

Replenished with food, they discussed what they would do next. "I think we should catalog the contents of the cave and the cabin," said Bran. "It's obvious no one has been here for years. I don't know who the owner was but maybe we'll find a clue when we open up everything. We'll try to do a neat job, so that nothing is really disturbed. What do you think?"

They started to stack the dishes and clean up.

"I think you're right. I'd like to open the trunk by the bed. Sometimes people wrap their things in newspaper. I think there's something in the paper that keeps the bugs away. If there are newspapers in there, we could get some dates to go on.

"Good idea," observed Bran. "I'll help get the trunk open for you then, I'll go and tackle the cave."

They put all the clean dishes back in the hutch, wiped the counter down and left the area better than they found it. Bran filled the reservoir in the stove with water from the pump, to heat for Night's bath later. This would be his surprise for her.

The trunk locks were stiff from disuse. Bran had to tap them lightly and apply a little pressure to the lid. It finally raised with a loud creaking. Since the hinges didn't break on opening, Bran tipped the lid back against the bed. The first shelf was sectioned in to small compartments. They lifted this out and set it on the bed. It was filled with an assortment of sewing supplies, some beaded necklaces and a sort of catchall of buttons and things. No newspapers!

Their real interest was in the contents of the main part of the trunk. Sunny quickly took out the first few things. "Look, these are baby clothes. What on earth would a baby be doing up here?" Sunny unfolded the delicate hand stitched white christening dress with matching cap. Its age made it look like rich cream in the glow of the lamps. Delicate hair-like embroidery decorated the neckline and the brim of the cap. There were tiny undershirts, flannel blankets and knitted sweaters.

The most unusual thing was a coat made out of wool scraps, all embroidered together and lined with a dark silky material. Immediately to Sunny's mind came the story of '*Joseph And His Coat Of Many Colors.*' This was a miniature version and was beautifully made.

"Bran, do you remember the story of '*Joseph And His Coat Of Many Colors*'?"

Bran had quit looking at the contents of the trunk as he

watched Sunny. In the light, her expression had taken on an ethereal beauty. As she fondled the baby clothes, she looked lovelier than the '*Madonna*'painting, "Beautiful, just beautiful," he responded to Sunny looking at her, not the coat she was admiring. At that instant he would have given anything to see a baby, with dark hair, nursing at her perfect breasts. His loins were stirring. Bran watched as Sunny unearthed the last remaining item of the trunk. On her knees, she lifted the garment up enough to recognize it for what it was.

Automatically, she hugged it to her body and looking up at Bran, her blue eyes liquid heaven, she whispered, "A wedding dress." Her mind saw Bran as her lover waiting to make her his bride, his dark, solemn look making promises to keep for the rest of their lives. She licked her lips sensually. Her eyes took on a dreamy look.

Her dream shattered as a frustrated, Bran croaked, "I've got to get out of here." Bran turned on his heels and hastily disappeared through the low door.

He stopped under the cave opening. Weakly leaning his hands against the rock wall with his head thrown back, he took deep breaths of fresh air. Ironically, he had exchanged his specter, the Raven, for sexual frustration.

In other circumstances, he would have been delighted to know he was no longer impotent, but years of ethics couldn't be discarded by caveman tactics. He was the boss: she was the employee, he was older, and had major hang-ups. He had a battered body, but by-god, one part of him was all right again.

At that moment, the radio started crackling indicating someone was trying to get through to them, or some other crew member in the backcountry needing them for a relay station. He took it up the rope ladder with him to get clear contact to hear who or what they wanted.

At first Sunny was startled as Bran turned and literally ran from the room. She then analyzed what she had been doing and grinned to herself. The old lip-licking trick had got to him again, only this time she had forgotten and had really meant it in a sensual way.

Her musing was cut short by a shout from the back room. "Night! Get your butt out here right now."

Oh boy, was that lover like, she thought. "Okay Bran, what is your problem?" her voice projected before her through the door.

Bran was coming down the ladder. "We've got to leave. While we got lots of rain here, they had a lightening bust up at Hozomeen, and no rain. Even the with the low ceiling, Desolation Lookout can see a glow over towards Copper Mountain. You've been ordered into the next boat up. They will bring your fire pack and pick you up at the Big Beaver boat landing. You'll probably overnight at Hozomeen and be ready at first light to go to the fire. I'll walk over with you, then come back here and close up. I've been ordered back to the station on stand-by."

Bran ran his fingers through his hair. "Damn! And double damn! I wanted to finish this job first."

Even as Bran was talking, Sunny sprung to action. Her pack was nearly ready, as she hadn't unpacked more than was immediately needed.

"Can I borrow your tarp? Mine is wet and still over the entrance hole. Here's the bag that it goes in and a clean garbage sack to stuff the whole wet thing in."

Sunny was efficiently sorting and packing and leaving some of the food for Bran.

"Sure, Night, and keep your flashlight out. It might get too dark before we get to Big Beaver."

Sunny grinned to herself. Bran just couldn't remember she had been doing this kind of thing for years now.

Bran collected some of his stuff to sort out on the table ready to go in his pack. He probably would sleep here and leave early in the morning.

"I have some room in my pack now that most of the food is gone. Do you want me to take anything out for you as proof of what we've found? It will be safe enough, as this pack doesn't go to the fire with me," asked Sunny. She turned to him.

Bran shrugged, "I'm not sure what to do, but why don't you take the wedding dress and maybe the baby cap and dress. I'm going to take this Delft pitcher and wrap the baby coat around it. I'll take a couple of the tools back there in the cave for evidence. We'll bring it all back when we come to finish cataloging." He arms swung wide indicating the contents of the room.

Sunny carefully did as she was told, then waited at the ladder for Bran to blow out all the lights and close the cabin door. He brought the lantern with him to see them out. They both gazed back towards the cabin for one last look. It was such a lovely little cabin. Going back up the ladder, they were on their way.

A few hours later, Bran arrived back at the cave. The lantern, which had been turned low, was still burning. He decided to fill it again before retiring for the night. Going back into the cabin, the room was still cozy warm and inviting. He could smell the aroma of biscuits yet. In fact, Bran set the lantern on the table, picked up a leftover one, spread some blueberry jam on it, then, downed it in two bites.

Even though it was getting late now, he finished putting things way and pumped a bucket of fresh water for a shave in the morning. Thinking of water reminded him he could have a bath with all the hot water left in the reservoir in the stove. He grinned.

Night was going to miss this treat. Remembering the old tub back in the cave, he retrieved it. He would only be able to get in it if he left his legs out. He filled the tub, scooping out a dipper full at a time from the reservoir. A little bit of cold water to get the temperature just right, and it was ready.

He stripped. His muscular arms and legs gleamed copper from the lantern light. The scars on his body were muted in the shadows. He swung his head forward, then backward, as he checked to see where the tub was as he lowered his buttocks into the water. As he did this the lamplight shown on his swinging hair, making his shadow resemble the god Mercury with wings on his head. He ginned at his fanciful thought.

Relaxing, he closed his eyes. God, this felt good. The water caressed his body. He grabbed the wine bottle from the table and tipping it up, finished the last dregs from it.

"Ah, a hot tub, lantern light, a sip of wine; but no thou," he murmured wishing his Night were here to scrub his back. When they both made contact again, he would have a talk with her. His thoughts rambled as he mussed. I really think I'm falling in love for the first time. I feel she's attracted to me, but with all my problems, can I let her take them on? I'll never know until I ask her.

Soaping his body, he started enjoying his bath. A bawdy Irish tune erupted, more on the loud side than on the musical. Water splashed on the floor. But who gives a damn, he thought as he slopped water under his armpits and around his backside.

Cleaning up his bath, he dumped the water down the drain muttering, "I sure hope it doesn't clog the drain from all the dirt." He retired to the bed. Minus the tarp, the bed seemed more comfortable than before. The dust smell didn't bother him. Over the years, he certainly had slept in worse places: in fact, terrible places.

Beside the bed was the night table, again crafted out of cedar. The drawer had been stuck tight when he had tried it before. It stuck a little now, but with some wiggling it pulled open. The heat in the cabin had probably dried out what little moisture there was he thought. Inside the drawer were several pencils, four black bound books and a bible.

Pulling out the top black book, he settled back to read thinking Abe Lincoln must have felt like this; lamplight to read by. The book was a diary. Bran proceeded to read an astounding account of history. Before he blew out the lantern, his life had been changed forever.

In the morning, he packed the four diaries, the bible and the baby coat with the Delft pitcher wrapped in it. The jam jar went in a plastic zip-lock bag. It would just spoil if left here. Ruin good blueberry jam? You have got to be kidding.

He decided to leave a list of the things Night and he were taking from the cabin. He made the list stating the things 'Night' Sunny Day had in her pack and the things Bran Donovan would have in his.

He hoped he and Night would be able to come back to do the cataloging, but if not, these things would be added to the list and maybe even brought back here. Bran walked over to the cedar bedside table. He put the list in the drawer. No mice could get at it in there.

He left the cabin tidy, collected Sunny's tarp and disassembled the rope ladder. When he came back here again, it would be with a better ladder for getting in and out of the cave. Piling rocks over the entrance mostly to keep the larger animals from making a home there, he started the climb back over the top of the cave area.

Going back down the trail, the first rays of sunlight were coming over the majestic Cascade Mountain range heralding a beautiful day. The staid man was deep in thought. The cawing ravens were heard as they settled in their favorite tree, watching the man as he walked down the trail and out of sight.

CHAPTER 13

BRAN'S REVELATION

Sunny was part of the crew grubbing the fire line. The borate plane had dropped a load on the fire slowing its progress a little. Normally, the Park Service would have just let the fire burn as part of nature, but this fire had gotten out of hand before they even had a chance to control it. It could go for miles and cross the Canadian border if they didn't do something to halt the progress. The crews were trying their best. The area seemed to have east of the Cascade Mountains conditions, getting very little rain during the summer months. The ground was very dry and dusty. It was dirty work to grub a fire line. The smoke and ashes in the air didn't help either.

Dirty, sweaty, with black streaks where she had wiped sweat away on her face, Sunny thought longingly of the bath Bran had been secretly preparing for her. She had seen him putting all that water into the stove's reservoir. Tonight, when the next crew came to take over for the shift, she would bathe even if she shocked the whole camp, ruined the ecology of the stream

they were camped by, and mosquitoes ate her whole body. She!
Would! Wash!

The days became a week before the fire was under control
and could be handled by the mop-up crew to watch the hot
spots. The tired, hungry, dirty crews were flown out by
helicopter to Hozomeen, where the fire base camp had been
set up. It felt so good to have a shower and sleep in a real bed,
even if it was just bunk beds and at least four people to a room.
Sunny couldn't have told you who else had been in the cabin,
she was so tired.

The trip down the lake by boat the next morning was
beautiful but uneventful. Nearing Big Beaver Campground,
she looked longingly up where the cave was. No sign of it existed,
only slide areas in numerous spots on the mountain. One was
probably it. She was about to tell one of the fellows about it
and was even pointing towards the area, when she had second
thoughts. It wasn't her job to tell anyone and have the whole
country overrunning the find. For all she knew, they might be
doing that already. She hoped not. Nothing would ever be the
same if they exploited it.

It was, however, a preserved piece of history. No one had
ransacked it and carried off all the treasures it held. So much
evidence of the history of this area was gone, either buried
under the lake or torn down in the name of progress.

The lack of conversation from the tired crew gave Sunny
time to think of Bran. She ached to be held and kissed by him.
She knew she shouldn't be having these thoughts: that was
fraternizing with the employees. If everyone did that, it would
be one big orgy all summer. Being thrown together the way
they were in their line of work, you shared a lot more than
normal office job contact. Sunny didn't know the teachers she
worked with for nine months of the years as well as she knew
some of the crew she only worked with for a few months in the
summer.

She even knew Bran better than his psychologist did. Bran
with his beat up body, his phobias, and his stoic image was a

fellow she could fall in love with given half a chance. Sunny, friend to all, wanted more than friendship for the first time in her life. For the last ten years, she had been the bridesmaid but never the bride. Why she even had a bride's dress in her backpack from the chest in the cabin she and Bran had been exploring.

She looked around at the boat full of her fire fighting comrades, and giggled to herself. What would they think if they knew she carried a bridal dress and baby clothes around with her? Good old Girl Scout: ready for anything. She giggled even louder this time. Over the noise of the boat engine no one heard her, and no one cared. They were too tired.

They reached Ross Lake Guard Station, hiked the mile long trail to the road and boarded the Crummy to take them back to Marblemount. During this time Sunny's muse never faltered from the time spent on the fire the last few days.

Looking the fire packs over, Sunny thought of all the stories she had heard about the fire fighters. The Pulaski tool for fighting fire was named for a fellow that had bullied his crew into a cave to save their lives. The fire was all around them. The crew had wanted to run, but he had known they couldn't outrun a wild fire. The cave just happened to be there to get into. It must have been terrible to have the fire raging all around the cave or maybe it was a mineshaft, and wondering if you were really going to survive.

When they reached the Ranger Station, a message to 'Night' was waiting for Sunny saying 'contact Bran'. Upon inquiring, she was told he was probably up in the Cascade Pass area, where his latest surveying was in progress. There was still some mining going on up there. Again, this was an area filled with history but most of it was gone through neglect and abandonment.

Her love of the outdoors was branching off into the historical part now that Bran had showed her how exciting just a blackened area on a rock wall could be. The rest of her day was spent cleaning fire packs and getting them ready to be used again should another fire ever go out of control.

Bran's work in the Cascade Pass area had taken him to a small meadow. A quiet stream meandered through it. It was his understanding, if he followed it for a bit he should come to a mineshaft. This area was all charted so his job was only to drive his brass stake, with its number on it, into the ground. He would then record the statistics in his ledger; the name of the mine and owner, plus what type of ore it produced.

Later he might do more in depth history, or the Park Naturalist would take over. It really was the Naturalist's job but he did whatever needed doing during the winter when things were slow.

He had walked away from the meadow into the dense forest following the stream. A splintering of golden rays worked itself through the forest canopy at this point, striking the stream up ahead. The stream curved to the east. The sun was at just the right angle to reflect the glint of mica in the pool of water, swirling off the low bank and cascading across shallow rocks. The result was a sparkling river of gold, or brook in this instance.

He wished he was like Night and carried a camera. The light was so intense he was sure it would have recorded the reflecting mica. It was the slight yellowness of the water that gave it the gold look. Plus, sometimes mica and iron pyrite was taken for gold: fool's gold. Mica broke up when handled, but some people still thought it was gold flakes. He vowed he would bring Night up here to see this. Lately, everything he thought of included Night. Not any of the fellows he worked with or his relatives, just Night.

After work, the Park Service wives had planned a corn feed and pie social. They felt it would ease the strain of this last week's fire, to let everyone eat all the corn on the cob they could eat. It was boiled in a huge crab pot on an open fire in the parking lot where the trucks were kept.

The trucks had been moved for the event having been washed after the fire and now were drying. Plenty of melted butter and hot coffee went along with this. To finish off the evening, there were several kinds of pie complete with ice cream to top them. Wild blackberry and high-mountain huckleberry seemed to be the favorites. The usual volleyball game would follow. Baseball was played more now that the days were longer. Played with a big softball, it was a game for everyone. Tonight, it seemed to be volleyball again.

It was at the crab pot, that Bran found Night. She was laughing at something someone had said. Butter dripped from her chin. It was all Bran could do to keep from grabbing her, licking the butter from her chin and taste the corn on her mouth. She had been gone a week and oh, how he had missed her.

Sunny saw him about then. Her laughter stopped. Her eyes lit up and she looked about to run into his arms. Instead, both realized where they were and a, "How's the corn," and "Have some corn," were the simultaneous greetings.

"I've got to talk to you," was the next double retort. The others, standing around the corn pot, laughed and asked if this was a comedy routine or could anyone join in. The laughter was at the expense of Sunny and Bran, but they didn't mind. Their message to each other had been received loud and clear. They continued to eat and talk to others but never were they separated by more than a few feet.

By telepathy, they seemed to get their pie and ice cream, and then maneuvered towards the motor home balancing both plates and coffee cup. Bran's picnic table was out there. They sat down at it to finish their pie and coffee.

Both looked at each other, like it had been years since they had been together. Between bites, Sunny laughingly told him how she had felt coming back from the fire camp, knowing she had a bridal gown and baby clothes in her backpack, while everyone else had only smelly fire clothing in theirs.

Evidently, he saw the humor because she got a smile out of him—her first one since seeing him tonight.

"Night, let's go for a drive. I really need to talk to you and I don't want to be interrupted by well meaning friends."

"Well, sure Bran, your car or mine?"

She just had to get another smile out of him. It worked, laughing Bran got up from the picnic bench and grabbed her gently by the cuff of the neck, shook her slightly as he led her to his car and helped her in. He quickly went back to the motor home to collect the diaries and the Bible.

Anxious to be on their way, Bran hurried back to his stylish car thankful he didn't have to ride in Night's little Volkswagen Beetle-bug car.

"Where do you want to go?"

"It's your show big guy. I certainly don't know what you have to tell me that couldn't be said right here," replied Sunny with and apprehensive look in her eyes.

Looking over at Night, Bran realized she was worried at his secretive manner.

"It's nothing to worry about, Night. I'm just excited at what I found after you left the cabin."

"Why didn't you say so? Here I was worrying about what may have happened here at the Ranger Station after I left you up at Big Beaver. What we found that day might have thrown everyone into a tizzy, although, no one mentioned it after I got back."

"I didn't tell anyone yet. Let's discuss this when we get to the wayside park down towards the town of Rockport."

Sunny kept quiet. This was the little park she had stopped at on her way to Marblemount the day she had come to work. It was a beautiful spot next to the highway and by the mighty Skagit River. Its huge maple trees leaning over the river gave it secluded spots in the shade. The farm to the north of the road gave it a peaceful feeling. The Episcopal Church at the end of the pasture gave it a quaint look. The gentle lapping of the river was soothing. This was a place to relax and tell stories

After letting a car pulling a trailer go by, Bran pulled the car off the road and into the roadside park, stopping near the first big maple. Getting out of the car, he retrieved a blanket and the sack, which he had put the diaries and the Bible in.

"Come on Night. Over here looks like a nice quiet spot."

Sunny followed Bran over to the tree and waited while he spread the blanket on the ground. They both found a comfortable spot on the blanket and slightly facing Night, Bran told his story.

"After I got back to the cabin, I used up your hot water for a bath." This got him a slap to the shoulder. "It really felt good!" he teased.

"I then opened that drawer in the night stand by the bed. In the drawer were four diaries and a Bible, which I brought out with me. I want you to read them for yourself because they are so interesting. I need to tell you what I think I found out by reading them."

Bran contemplated his words carefully.

"This couple that owned the cabin had a baby. This baby was called Joseph because of that '*Coat of Many Colors*' we found. His father made him a cradle. As you know from all the things in the cabin, this man was quite a craftsman. That cradle was made of cedar wood, pitched and pegged to hold it together. Its hood was shaped and carved like a raven. The rockers rocked just the opposite from most cradles. Looking from the side, it looked like the legs of the raven extended to capture something with the carved feet curled down, talons extended. This kept the cradle from rocking too far. Made this way, a person could strap it on their back, Indian fashion."

Engrossed in this story, Sunny still couldn't help but ask, "How do you know so much about this cradle?"

"Now don't interrupt," smiled Bran knowing more about this story than Night did.

He continued, "The baby's mother was a seamstress from back East and sewed all the baby clothes. One thing was a rabbit skin bunting. That's like a sack with a hood. I know this because

I've seen both it and the cradle." Bran ended his narration like a revelation, his eyes shining in the waning light.

Sunny, slightly confused said, "Where did you find those? The cabin wasn't big enough for me to miss something as big as a cradle."

"I didn't see them at the cabin. My Great-grandfather and his brother had a cradle like that. The bunting was theirs too."

"Bran, I'm very confused. Explain yourself!"

"I'm not sure I can explain it all, but let me tell you just a little more about what I read in the diaries. It's sad, but evidently the man was attacked by a bear and badly injured. The last entry was dated October 25, 1889 said his wife was taking him out to get medical help for his injuries. Now, the mystery is how did the cradle and the bunting come to belong to my Great-grandfather and his brother? What happened to this family?"

"Lord, I don't know but I can hardly wait to read the diaries."

"There's still one more surprise I found in the Bible when I finally got around to opening it after reading the diaries by lantern light." Bran dug around in the sack and came up with the Bible. He reverently opened it. He looked inside the cover and pulled out a picture.

"Who do you think this is?"

Sunny took the picture in her hand. The light was getting dark, but not bad enough for her to see that it was a wedding picture. She recognized the wedding dress. After all, she'd had it in her backpack for a week. But it was the man that caught her attention. He was about the age Bran was now. He had a beard, but there was no mistaking who he was. "My god Bran, it's you!"

"Correct! Well, not really correct, but yes, he looks just like I do after a week on the trail. He, also, looks just like my Great-grandfather in a picture I saw of him with a beard. Great-grandfather usual never wore a beard. I think he had just come off a freighter."

"What do you think all of this, means?" a baffled Sunny asked.

"There's a story I've heard over all these years, but at the time I thought it was like all the other myths I've lived with all my life. Great-grandfather and his brother were twins. Well, in those days twins were thought to bring bad luck to the tribe. Now you realize this was almost a hundred years ago. The story goes that one of the twins was delivered from the Water Spirit namely, the Skagit River; therefore, one of them was like a God to the tribe. They had to take very good care of this little God so the Water Spirit wouldn't get angry and take the fish away. So—one of these twins is the baby of the Water Spirit—. Guess who?"

"Great-grandfather?" Sunny shook her head in a yes gesture as she delivered this exclamation.

"Right the first time, if my calculations are correct. I need to go talk to my Great-grandfather who's still alive and very sharp on his good days. He's in a rest home down below. Would you like to come along?"

"I'd love to, if we can work it out. This centenarian Great-grandfather of yours really has me curious. Meanwhile, it looks like I have some every interesting reading to do."

Playfully, she got up and ruffled his hair while stepping towards the car. Bran grabbed her leg and giving a playful tug, sent her sprawling on top of him.

"Ohmph! For a pint size you're heavy," he gasped as the air was expelled out of his lungs.

Still half on top of him, she told him, "You know Bran, strange thing are happening here. I'm the one who usually babbles on, but lately I'm thinking you've kissed the *Blarney Stone* pulling my leg with wild stories."

A stout laugh from Bran issues forth. "You're right Night. I've been a quiet guy up until I met you. But I'm not pulling your leg about the stories. You bring out something in me. I'm not sure if it's just a cold sweat from a virus, or the *hots* for your body, but yeah, *Old Stone Face,* is talking more. Could be the blarney finally coming out in me."

With a sparkle in her eyes, Sunny said, "I've always

wondered what nut case would want to kiss a cold old stone and now I'm going to get a taste of that cold old '*Blarney Stone*' myself." And with that quip, she rained kisses on the not-so-old rock's cheeks, his neck and even his hands as they tried to ward off this ray of sunshine, scuffling with him on the blanket.

"Ah, come on Night. Quit that or you're going to get more than you've bargained for."

With that threat issued, Bran flipped her over onto the grass. In the twilight, Sunny found herself looking up at teasing black eyes. The black eyes drew closer and a dreamy look appeared. The kiss was long and hot. Sunny reveled in the sensuous kiss as Bran deepened it still further if that was possible.

Low moans issued forth from Sunny as her hands stole up under Bran's shirt. Those same hands started to delicately rub his back. Trying not to flinch every time her tiny fingers found a Keloid scar, Bran slowly rolled her over on top of him. Sunny lifted her head to bury her next kiss under his ear. How could this be so titillating? His body hardened. Bran moaned, "Night, if you don't stop this now, I'm in big trouble."

Sunny, barely hearing his plea realized they were both in big trouble if one or the other didn't put a brake on it. With one more big smacking kiss on his cheek, she rolled off him and sat up.

Bran rolled onto his stomach groaning. Burying his head in his arms, then turning his head slightly to look at her, he said, "Do you know you touched my scars? No one has ever touched my scars while I've been awake."

"Oh Bran, I'm so sorry. Did I hurt you?" An ever sensitive, Sunny, was crushed.

"No, no I didn't mean that. I meant I didn't go screaming off to never-never land. I am aching though but you're not supposed to know that. Let's go home."

Getting up they dusted grass and leaves from their clothes. Sunny helped Bran fold the blanket. Bran handed her the sack with the diaries and Bible in it. Walking back to the car, Bran removed some leaves from Night's clothes and a twig from her hair, an intimate gesture he wouldn't have done just a few short, weeks ago.

Reaching the car, he opened the door for her, then going around the car, he crawled in on the driver's side.

"Before we go back to the station, again you need to know, I haven't had a chance to tell anyone about the cabin yet. The fire kept everyone pretty busy. I intended to, but now I'd like to do a little more investigating so I can present a full version of the find and not have evidence lost or destroyed before I find out the truth of the story."

"I feel that way too, Bran. I won't tell anyone either."

She then proceeded to tell him more about the fire and her trip down the lake. Bran pulled out onto the highway going back towards the Ranger Station. She may think she's a babbling brook but to him her voice was like the tinkling of a stream over rocks in the quiet of the woods, very soothing. This thought reminded Bran about his week, and the gold colored stream. He would tell her when there was a break in the conversation, if there was a break.

CHAPTER *14*

SUNNY READS DIARIES

The four days that followed were busy ones for the whole Ranger Station. Fire equipment came down from Hozomeen by way of a truck through Canada. All equipment was cleaned, repaired and put in its place ready for any emergency it might be needed for.

Personnel took regular days off, while others resumed their normal activities waiting for their days off. The Naturalist came back from his school, freeing Bran from those duties. This left him more time to investigate the mystery of what happened to the Donovan family of the 1800's. And just where did the name Donovan come from since it was his name too? His dad had come straight from Ireland. Of course it was a good old, Irish name.

He haunted the libraries of Skagit County, the museums, and the newspapers. He was hampered slightly by certain newspapers that had been sent to the Washington State Library to be microfilmed in a State grant project. He interviewed old-timers still living.

This proved to be very interesting and a lot of information he got, he could use in writing up the mining of Skagit Valley and surrounding areas of the Park. He did more interviews from those leads. He was already familiar with the cassette taped interviews the Park Service had on file from old-timers, now most of them dead.

The best lead came when the King County Library system reported they had copies of the microfilmed newspapers Bran was looking for. This would require a trip to Seattle.

Meanwhile, during this same period of time, Sunny worked like a Trojan during the day, and at night read the diaries. She didn't see Bran, but knew they had a date to see his great-grandfather during her days off.

The diaries transported her to another time and of another world. An avid reader anyway, this was better than dessert after a meal and not nearly as fattening. She learned of crossing an ocean in the eyes of a little girl and made a note of the ship and year for Bran. She learned of a young lady's sorrow at losing her family and friends to sickness and her fiancée to the sea. There was the too tired feeling after days of work in the sweat—house sewing clothes to earn barely enough to just eat. The diaries took her from the East Coast, to the West Coast and eventually to the Skagit Valley.

Here the diaries changed from a frightened young girl to a blossoming woman, madly in love with her husband. Sunny, thought it was so romantic for Rafe to have had rings made alike from the gold that had been mined by him. From the diaries, Sunny learned how to make lye for homemade soap. Skin animals and tan the hides while canning the meat for the winter, using every bit of the killed animal.

She read about the hardship of growing vegetables. Getting hay for the mule, plus more vegetables, from the McMillan Ranch, then drying the vegetables or canning them for the winter months. The meals didn't sound too diversified, but the lovemaking brought roses to Sunny's cheeks. Did they really do that in those days?

It was at this point, Sunny read about the baby, the clothes and the famous cradle. The way Katy described their baby made Sunny feel something was missing in her life. Sometimes, Sunny opened her locker and had run her hands down the material of the wedding dress, or even looked for a seam the young Katrina had mentioned. She loved the romantic name of Katrina. Katy seemed too modern in Sunny's estimation.

Sunny's imagination often put her in Katy's shoes and she lived much of the story through the diaries. She glossed over the romantic spots not having much to compare it with. When she came to the end and Rafe most likely was dying from the bear attack, Sunny was crying her eyes out.

A depressed Sunny went to work the last day before her days off. She really felt like the 'Night' Bran called her. Even the crew noticed her quietness and red eyes.

"Did you lose your best friend or did they order you to work with the villain, Darth Vader again?" came the teasing remark.

"You're partly right, but mostly it was the book I've been reading. Tomorrow I'm going with Darth Vader to see his great grandfather. Mr. Donovan had given me the honor, on my day off, of visiting this distinguished gentleman. I'll really have a story to tell my kindergarten class when I go back to work this fall."

The crew noted she said her day off, which looked like work to them. With these thoughts of a day with Bran, Sunny smiled back at her peers making them feel the day was brighter now that their Sunny Day was smiling again. This crew liked each other and a bad day for one meant a bad day for all.

CHAPTER 15

GREAT-GRANDFATHER MOSES

Today was the day! Sunny wasn't sure what she should wear. Her meager wardrobe wasn't the height of fashion here. Those clothes were at home. She chose a turquoise gauze dress she had brought with her because it packed well and was cool. She tied it with a sash belt. Again, all she had were strap sandals, as heel shoes would have been ridiculous to bring up here. She didn't like the way she looked today, but it was time to meet Bran outside at his car. With butterflies in her stomach, she went out.

Bran was leaning against his car. At the sight of him, Sunny skipped down the couple of steps as lightly as a butterfly would, and approached Bran with her hands out to take his. He was so handsome with his black cowboy boots shining, his tight jeans hugging his lean hips. His long-sleeved western shirt was rolled up a couple of turns on his arms to show a watch with a turquoise studded band. His belt buckle and ring matched his watch. He looked like he was from Colorado's turquoise country now.

With their hands coupled, they stood looking at each other appreciating the sight.

"Come on, you beautiful gal with the turquoise eyes, let me put you in the car."

Looking him over and smiling up at him, she replied.

"You just do that you handsome man with turquoise jewels all over you."

Neither was used to compliments from the opposite sex, both smiling rather shyly when he did just that.

The trip to the retirement home where Bran's Great-grandfather resided was filled with the exchanging of news about what they had learned these last few days. On hearing Bran needed to go to Seattle after they visited his Great-grandfather, Sunny offered to go with him. She invited him to dinner with her parents. Lord only knew what her parents would think when she called home on such short notice. Things weren't pretentious at her home. Her mother would figure out a good wholesome meal, probably using the new bread-maker Sunny had given her for Mother's Day.

Her folks might not be pretentious, but now that the *'flower children'* days were gone, her mother liked any gadget that helped a woman cope with a job and family. A delicious pot of beans in the crock-pot and homemade bread, dripping with margarine, would be wonderful. She would suggest it to her mother, as already her mouth was watering for it.

Her mother would then blow all this nutritious food for some high calorie ridden rich dessert that would shorten your life by just looking at it. Her beautiful petite mother couldn't resist a good dessert and her high metabolism seemed to burn it off. She giggled out loud at this.

"What's that giggle for after that pensive study of the road for the last ten minutes."

"I've been thinking about what my family will think when I call them at such short notice for our trip to Seattle. The giggle was thinking of that fancy dessert you'll be served. It will be so gooey and dripping with icing or whipped cream, you'll feel like a cream puff just trying to eat it."

"I'm getting sick just listening to you describe it. Give me the European style, just wine and cheese and thee, any day. Especially, the thee," leered a grinning, Bran.

Sunny was surprised at the unexpected flirting of the stoic Bran Donovan. They arrived at the rest home. Bran was told his Great-grandfather had had a bad night, but insisted on seeing Bran anyway. As Bran promised not to stay too long or tire the old man, the attendant smiled them on their way to his room.

The entered the ground floor room. It was kind of a sitting room with a bed, bathroom and a very small kitchenette. A patio out the sliding door had a chaise lounge to recline on. Flowers hung in baskets with the suspicion of a few vegetables growing in the containers out there. Sunny recognized Tom Thumb tomatoes or the size that was good for one bite.

Sunny quietly stayed in the background. Bran approached his Great-grandfather, who was propped up with several pillows, while reclining on the bed. Moses was dressed, but a crocheted lap robe had been thrown over his legs. He had been watching television but clicked it off with the remote control as they came in. Putting the remote control down he put out his hands and Bran took them in his.

Bran spoke, "Dear Great-grandfather, do you recognize me today?"

The very old wizened man, showing very prominent cheekbones, his nose straight and fine, glanced at the young man. His eyes, even at this advanced age were very piercing under heavy brows. He spoke in a very ancient whispering voice.

"You are the son of my daughter's daughter. You have the ancient look. In every generation there is a look. Like me, you carry that look."

"You are right, dear Great-grandfather. I carry the look. And now I will tell you a story of that look."

Bran started the story and as Sunny listened she was amazed

at this modern man. Before her eyes, he became the ancient storyteller of the ceremonial fires. The room seemed to become darker and Bran seemed to glow. And so the story started.

"In the long ago time, when your life, dear Great-grandfather, was just beginning, there lived a miner and his wife. They lived in this house at the entrance to a cave in the mountains, near the headwaters of the Skagit River. They were a God-fearing people, very good, and lived off the land. They had a little son. The Spirit of the Bear came to get this man. They escaped to the river trying to get away from the Bear Spirit. It was there; the River Spirit took them to live with her forever more, protecting them from the Bear. The River Spirit saved the child and gave him to our people of the Skagit to raise. In doing so, she promised to keep the fish running. Our people raised the boy as one of their own, thinking he was the son of the River Spirit. Do you remember this little boy, dear Great-grandfather?"

Sunny sat there entranced, listening to this tale. Was this man reincarnated Indian of olden days, or was it the Gaelic tongue speaking? Bran's voice had taken on a sing-song quality, but the deep Irish baritone reverberated throughout the story.

Old Moses, keeping to the quality of the atmosphere that had been created, answered the question his great-grandson had just projected into the room.

In a musical, whispering voice he said, "Yes, I remember this story. My father was the one who brought this baby to our home. This son of the River Spirit was raised as a twin. Twins were thought to be bad luck for a tribe. Another tribe wouldn't take a twin into their home and bring bad luck to all of them. It was necessary for our tribe to trick other tribes, and also the Evil Spirits that may have tried to steal the son of the River Spirit away. We would have lost our bounty from the mighty river if the baby had been spirited away."

Great-grandfather tiring a little closed his eyes. He then took a deep breath before continuing.

"These babies slept in the same cradle. The cradle the River

Spirit's son came to them in. They were dressed alike and treated alike. All during our growing-up years, the river gave forth its fish. Our tribe was never hungry. I know who these children were. They were Noah, may his Spirit rest in peace, and myself. My brother, Noah thought he was the son of the River Spirit, but his secret Spirit was the owl. I know the River Spirit's baby was myself. My secret Spirit's is the mighty salmon."

The old man gave the younger one a nod.

"It was bad luck to kill your secret Spirit's image. I was never the fisherman, but the hunter for the tribe. I did participate in the ceremony to the salmon. My Spirit was most powerful at that time. It has save me many times. Once I nearly drowned in a boating accident but the salmon came, circled me a couple of times, then led me to the closest point of land. I might have headed in the opposite direction if they hadn't shown me the way."

He stuttered slightly, overcome with emotion. "When I was near death a few years back, we nearly lost our salmon run. I've been preparing for death ever since, so that won't happen again when I die."

This long dialogue tired the old man. He quietly closed his eyes and breathed deeply for a few minutes. As he regained his strength, his eyes slowly opened.

Bran's deep stirring voice spoke.

"So, the story is true that has been passed down for generations? There was a River Spirit's baby and that baby turned out to be you. Did you hear me when I said this baby was born to a white man and his wife?"

"Yes, I am slowly hearing what you are saying. However, the baby was still delivered from the River Spirit."

"That is true Great-grandfather. You have always had the great, River Spirit with you, but would you like to know what your name was before you were delivered to the tribe?"

"I am Moses Swift-River, just Moses Swift now. I have another Indian name and I have a secret spirit name. I've also been called a few other names not so nice. What is one more name to me?" There was a raspy chuckle from the old man, showing humor in his long life.

Bran smiled at this display of amusement from his dignified ancestor.

"I will tell you anyway, Great-grandfather. Many moons from now, when you go to the Great Creator in the sky, you will at least know all there is to know about yourself. Your parents have been trying to tell you through the Raven to me. I must tell you so the Raven will leave me in peace. Your name is Joseph Donovan!"

At this the old man started, his piercing black eyes looked deep into Bran's.

Bran continued, "I know! This is very strange. The whole story is strange. My name of Donovan couldn't even be related to your name of Donovan unless it was traced back to the old country of Ireland. Your father, Rafe Donovan, was a gold miner and later, a trapper. He married a Dutch girl, Katrina denBerg. You were their only child. There is a wedding picture of them. You and I look like Rafe Donovan. Katy Donovan appears to be blond-haired. It seems the Gods wanted the name of Donovan to continue and sent, N-n, er," Bran stuttered, "Sunny Day to me to unlock the secret."

Bran gestured towards Sunny. At the mention of Sunny Day, the old man looked puzzled.

"I know. Another strange happening, this lovely lady is named Sunny Day."

"Good Indian name," grunted the old man.

Bran ignored the reference to Sunny being Indian. It was a logical conclusion with her black hair, plus it was a compliment from this revered relative. Bran continued his story.

"She found the first evidence of the cave. The ravens did the rest. When you are up to the task, I will let you read your mother's diary. It described your cradle very well. Whatever happened to the cradle?"

"Our father had decreed the cradle always go to the first born son, thinking he would probably be the carrier of the

River Spirit. Noah had a son first, so the cradle went to his side of the family. My father didn't know that until I die the River Spirit's protection, will not be passed on."

He thought a moment and continued, "In this day and age, I doubt if anyone even believes in the Spirits, although there has been a revival in our people wanting to know more about their Indian ancestry."

Moses looked Bran in the eye, "I'm not sure how many first-born sons there have been to pass the cradle on to."

Bran filed this in his head to pursue later.

"Dear Great-grandfather, do you think you can think of yourself as a white man named Joseph Donovan?"

A long pause issued forth. The old man was either gathering strength or thinking about his answer. At last the whispering voice concluded, "I would be proud of the name of Donovan. You are a great-grandson to be proud of. However, your blood has been mixed with the whites ever since I married your white Great-grandmother. All of your side of the family have continues of marry whites."

He gave Bran a knowing look.

"We've all gotten so scattered around the world with the wars, it was only the Skagit that finally pulled us back home to die and be buried. I've been and Indian for nearly a hundred years. I was raised an Indian. I think like an Indian. I will keep my proud Indian name. I will die like and Indian, but when I am dead, you can put all my many names on my grave. I'll leave you a written list as you probably can't spell my Indian ones."

Saying this, he put his college graduate, helicopter pilot, war hero, great-grandson down a peg or two in ability.

"We will leave you to rest Great-grandfather. I will be back to see you."

"Thank you, Bran the Raven, for coming. I will think about your revelation. I think you have just released me from the River Spirit. The fish will continue to run when I die. When you come again, bring your Sunny Day with you. A man could hardly do better than have sunny days all year long."

"Amen, dear Great-grandfather, Amen!" chuckled Bran as Sunny's face turned as red as the setting sun.

Bran and Sunny left the rest home to go back to the car.

"What a wonderful old man that was back there. He seemed so bright and gentle."

"Don't let that air of fragility fool you. That old man was one hell-raiser in his youth. I guess those two twins ran wild without too much discipline. The tribe was afraid they would anger the River Spirit and wasn't too sure which twin was which, either. During the First World War he enlisted. His exploits were not only heroic, but notorious. Uncle Noah went, too: two peas in a pod. Uncle Noah died years ago."

Bran looked up at the sky as if his uncle was up there.

"Later, Great-grandfather worked the oil fields, even bummed around some freighters that went to the South Pacific. My Great-grandmother finally caught and tamed him in Seattle. They moved back to the Skagit to run a neighborhood grocery and service station. He's had three wives, you know."

They reached the car. It was a beautiful day so they stood there leaning against the car fender talking.

"His first wife, one of the tribe, died soon after they were married. They must have had his first child at that time. He died years ago, too. My great-grandmother, a white lady, had two children before she died: one being my grandmother. He's out lived another wonderful Indian lady that I called Great-grandmother. When he dies, he will be buried next to her in the Indian Cemetery near Marblemount."

Bran's expression was thoughtful.

"You know, we all thought we had a right to be buried in that cemetery if we wanted to. Now that the truth is known, our family being adopted Indian and all, I wonder what our 'right's' really are? Do I still have fishing rights? Burial rights? Wow! This will take some thinking on."

He opened the car door and helped Sunny in. Going around the car, he got in the driver's side. Sunny watched him shake his head slightly and another, "Wow!" was exclaimed.

They headed back up the beautiful Skagit Valley with its rolling hills lining the fertile valley to the sides and the white topped rugged ones framing the forward view to the east towards Marblemount. Sometimes they followed the river, sometimes they straddled the valley with the farms on either side. Both people were thoughtful as they enjoyed the trip home.

CHAPTER *16*

SUNNY'S FAMILY

The next day was raining as Sunny and Bran, headed down river to Seattle.

"I called my folks last night. They are absolutely thrilled to be meeting you, although they've only heard bad things bout you." Sunny looked sideways at Bran, apprehensively, to see how he was taking this little bit of news.

"Bad things about me? How come?"

Sunny laughed enjoying Bran's discomfort.

"No seriously, how come?" Bran didn't like the idea of being on the bad side of Night's parents, having already forgotten she had said they were thrilled.

"Well, at the start of the summer all you did was glare at all of us but me in particular. I never got a smile out of you until I said you could call me 'Night'. Why did you call me Night?"

"I really don't know why Sunny never registered as your name. You were always just 'Night when I thought of you. I couldn't have said if it was your first name or your last name.

You were just my *'Night'n day, you are the one,'*" crooned Bran with words this time.

An incredible look flashed across his face. "Well, I'll be damned! That's the song I've been humming since you licked your lips at me, that time at the potluck, orientation dinner. It's been driving me crazy that old Cole Porter song, just out of reach in my mind."

Now to test the word, Bran sang the whole song to Sunny, as she sat enthralled having a love song sung to her. This man could have made his living singing, his voice so resonant and sensuous.

"Bran, that was lovely. It didn't matter that you called me Night, but I swear I'll change my name after that wonderful song you just sang to me."

"I think your parents would have something to say about that," ginned Bran.

"You think so? My parents' brains function like that. They would think it very romantic to be named because of a song. I was probably named after a summer day in June after my parents had made love in a meadow. That's the kind of parents I have."

The world-weary man could feel his ears burning at this. He now knew more that he wanted to know about Night's parents. Changing the subject slightly, he explained the song.

"That's was an old song my father used to sing, probably of his era. He knew some great ones, if you could get him off the raunchy Irish songs. I swear, he knows every song written if it's a little off color. Once he hears a song, he never forgets it and can sing and play it back almost immediately."

Bran sighed at his next revelation. "When I was getting well in the hospital he would come in and start singing every ribald song he knew, and had all the Vets singing and clapping soon. Even the nurses loved it, but their faces would turn red if they stuck around too long."

Sunny laughed at this, thinking her face would turn red too, if she heard those songs. She had led a sheltered life Bran continued, "My mother was forever trying to reform him. I think he goes to church with her just so he can say the 'bad' word to her legally. If you listen carefully, he enunciated every one of those words in her ear just to see her blush. He teases her unmercifully."

By now Sunny was laughing so hard, she had to dab her eyes with a tissue. This was the stoic Bran? This was the man that couldn't smile? The old iceman had melted, she thought, and she loved it.

Not knowing what Sunny was thinking, and with concern in his voice, Bran asked. "Will you folks wonder why I was such an old grouch?"

This was a man, not long out of the shell he had built around himself.

"No Bran. They won't care. My folks will be trilled to see you because they like people. If anything, they will want to try to help you because I said you couldn't smile. That's a challenge to them. If they knew I liked you, and only you, they would be even more thrilled because I've never had someone that was more than just a friend before."

"Really! Never! I'm more than just a friend?"

In his heart he knew this, but to hear it from Night went to his head like a glass of fine bourbon. Now that he'd gotten rid of some of his phobias with her help, she left him dizzy and weak. Every feeling was new to him again. He'd learned to trust again, feel again, and love, maybe for the first time. He felt he needed to touch her now and then just to make sure she was real.

Thinking those thoughts, he reached over and gently touched her hand. Sunny waited for some kind of declaration from Bran. However, she waited in vain as Bran was still getting used to a woman liking him, let alone more than liking him. He gloried in it for awhile before he remembered, he had called his own parents last night, too.

"I called my folks last night, also. They'll be up here next week to help with the preparations for Great-grandfather's centennial birthday party. I told my folks I had something very important to tell them when they get here. They were going to meet the girl that was instrumental in helping me with this good news. It was strange though. Both were on different phones and there was total silence on their end. I thought they would be interested in the news about Great-grandfather and all I got was silence."

Bran glanced at Night. "They did quietly say they would like to meet you."

"Did you phrase your sentence just as you told me, or did you mention your Great-grandfather's news?" Sunny moved forward and turned towards Bran, so she could see his face as he drove.

Bran removed his hand from Sunny's and gripped the steering wheel. A light dawned on Bran's face.

"You're right. I told them word for word like I told you. Ah ha! They think I'm going to tell them I'm in love with a girl named Night and want to marry her. Right?"

Sunny sat back in her seat and hung her head. "I'm sure that was exactly what they were thinking, Bran, and I'm sorry. Your folks have enough news coming to them without that ruining their day."

"Ruin their day! My god Night! Do you really want to know what they would do? That would make them the happiest people in the world, my sister the second. You don't know what I've put my family through."

He quickly glanced over at her again, patting her hand.

"For bringing me out of my shell, those people will love you the rest of your life and will probably use some spell to work after life, also."

"Yeah, well, okay, but I'm sorry I put you in such a spot now, Bran."

"Put me on the spot? Just a minute." Seeing a rest area sign ahead, Bran signaled as he pulled into the long lane leading to the rest stop. Looking for a parking place, he drove on around the buildings to the far end of the parking area.

There under a stand of graceful Hemlock trees, he pulled the 'Z' car in. Turning the car off, he unbuckled the seat belt, then turned toward Sunny.

"Now, you did not put me on the spot. I would love to marry you right this minute. I would ask you here and now, if I thought I was man enough for you. I'm enough of a burden to myself and family without inflicting myself on the woman I love."

Sunny unbuckling her seat belt started to glow from inner happiness.

"You love me? You'll marry me? I accept. I love you, you big ox. I love you, your scars, phobias and all."

She launched herself at him, no mean feat in a sports car. He caught her deep in his arms. He lowered the seat to a reclining position. The kisses they exchanged and the feelings they radiated were undeniable. Only broad daylight and a public place stopped them from continuing the loving action to its natural conclusion.

The barking of a leashed dog, brought Bran out of his passion, induced trance.

"Night love, we have a job to do even though I like this job the best," giving her a loud smacking kiss.

Looking up at her face, Bran appreciated the raven wing hair swinging around Night's face. His Raven was becoming a sign of love, not fear of what might happen next.

"I'm sorry. I forgot everything. Did you really mean to ask me to marry you or am I jumping to conclusions because I would like it to be true?"

"Believe me Night, I want this to be true, but I will say, it's taken me by surprise. Until I said it, I didn't really believe it. But I do love you. You're all I think about anymore."

"Thank you, Bran the Raven."

Giving him a sweet kiss on the cheek, she moved off of him and onto her side of the car. She patted his leg as he moved the seat back to its upright position.

"Now let's get to Seattle before the library closes. We both want to solve the mystery of what happened to your relatives all those years ago."

Bran and Sunny smiled at each other often on the rest of the trip to Seattle. The usual heavy traffic kept Bran on his toes, so conversation was kept to a minimum. Near the library complex, parking was horrendous. They finally found parking in a lot where they wouldn't have to run out and feed the parking meter every hour.

The microfilmed newspapers they needed for their research were not many due to the fact they knew about what dates to look for. There also, weren't that many different newspapers to look at because there weren't that many being published in the 1800's. They started with the date of the last entry in the diaries. Finally, in one of the oldest publishers, the Argus of Mount Vernon, they found the newspaper article they were looking for, but had hoped it wouldn't be such bad news.

About six months after the last entry in the diary, a newspaper article stated: *A man and a woman had been found, hands tied together, caught in the huge logjam on the Skagit River. The couple had drowned but the bodies were in pretty good condition due to the cold temperature of the river during the winter. After no identification could be found, no foul play was suspected, and no one came to claim the bodies the city of Hamilton had given them a nice funeral and plots in the Hamilton Cemetery. This had been paid for with the gold nugget rings, the couple, were still wearing at the time.*

With tears in her eyes, Sunny consoled Bran.

"I'm so glad they were given a Christian burial by the good people of Hamilton."

Bran put his arm around Sunny's shoulder.

"That's all right Night. It happened a long time ago. It's just fresh news to you and me since we've been the ones to do the investigating."

"I know Bran. I just feel I know them so well after reading the diaries. Come on. Let's go back to Everett to my folk's home. Mom and Dad will cheer us up; or come to think of it—we'll cheer them up if we give them our good news."

Even though they were whispering, they were getting a few strange looks. They copied the articles they needed, then returned the microfilm negatives back to the reference desk.

The trip out of Seattle was just in time for the Boeing traffic. There were people going home from other jobs and companies, but around Seattle, the traffic was known as the Boeing traffic, from the mighty air craft company doing business from Seattle. This traffic would be heavy all the way to Everett and beyond due to the many people needed to run the huge company. Sunny related this information to Bran as he impatiently navigated the freeway.

"You can tell I've been in the mountains too long," grimaced, Bran, as he hit the steering wheel with the palm of his hand, while completely stopped at one point.

They reached the Everett turn-off to Sunny's home. Another half-hour and they pulled up to the well cared for farmhouse. A wrap-around porch had a chained wooden swing on it: good for reading and swinging, on a warm day, Sunny told Bran. Flowers bloomed everywhere in well tended beds. Hereford cattle were seen in the far pasture. Some chickens came running up expecting a handful of grain.

"Sorry chicks, I don't have anything," crooned Sunny as if they were pets.

Bran followed her into the house.

"I'm home, Mom!" called Sunny.

A miniature whirlwind came out of the kitchen. To Bran's eyes, Night and her mother could well be sisters. The same long, dark hair, and the same petite size. Sunny's mother, wore her dress long with bulky sandals, while Night looked modern in her jeans, plaid shirt, tennis shoes, and windbreaker to keep the rain off. Sunny quickly introduced Bran to her mother, Margarete. Although, pleased to meet him, the two women had much to talk about. After giving him a cup of coffee made from freshly ground coffee beans, he was soon ignored.

Letting them talk, Bran wandered outside to the porch swing. He knew Night wanted to tell both of her parents at the same time about their engagement. Engagement! Now there was a hard word for him to say.

Rocking slightly in the swing and sipping coffee, he had time to think about this new development in his life. He was apprehensive. What if he became manic again? Could he put Night through that? Where was that stiff backbone, they all told him he had too much of?

As Bran contemplated the pros and cons of life with Night, a sharp looking green MG British car growled up the driveway, shifted down in a typical sports car style, then screeched to a halt in the garage. The car was old but in excellent condition. Bran could appreciate that as he had spent all those hours restoring his 240 Z car.

Bran watched a man, presumably, Night's dad, come out of the garage, lope along and athletically hop onto the porch. He was dressed in a neatly tailored brown suit, with a beige shirt, and loosened off-centered tie, complete with—tennis shoes? His slightly curly, long hair was tied back in a ponytail. He was a Mel Gibson look-alike.

"Hi! I'm Ferris Day. I take it you're Bran Donovan, Summer's friend?"

"I guess I am, but I had forgotten she had another name on top of all the others she has."

Now Ferris looked confused for a minute then he smiled at Bran.

"I guess most people call her Sunny, but to us she is Summer: her given name."

Bran laughed, "And to me she's Night. She has as many names as my Great-grandfather." Waving his hand as in *'don't ask'*. "It's a long story. Let's go in and see if the girls are still talking a-mile-a-minute."

Going in the house the whirlwinds attacked Ferris. He laughingly grabbed one and whirled her around saying, "How'd your day go Mugs?"

Then grabbing the next one, whirled her around saying, "How's my best girl?"

This ritual was so natural and dance like, Bran knew it had happened many times before. Both women talked at once, but he seemed to understand them from long practice.

It was over the gooey dessert that Bran and Sunny exchanged conspirator glances. I told you so; was Sunny's look. Bran's was; how do you eat this stuff?

Laughing, Sunny said, "Mom and Dad, Bran and I have something we'd like to tell you."

The parents exchanged glances and then looked expectantly at the two younger people.

"Bran and I would like to announce our intentions to marry sometime soon."

A glow seemed to come over the two parents. A moment later and incredulous look came over their faces. Both jumped up as Sunny stood. They rushed around the table to enclose her in a threesome bear hug. Bran slowly rose to his feet, thankful to leave the gooey dessert right where it sat.

Again, everyone seemed to talk at once but understood each other anyway. Bran endured a hardy backslap meant to be a congratulation. He didn't lose his wind but it was a close thing. The girls wandered off to plan or whatever women do. Bran was left with a sharp-eyed father to contend with.

"Come into the study. I've got some good brandy to celebrate with."

Bran followed dutifully. Ferris hand him a small glass of the heady drink.

"Now, what are your intentions towards my little girl?"

Bran had heard about this ritual and had laughed in the past. Now, here it was and it didn't seem like a laughing matter to him. He was royally put on the hot spot now.

"Sir. This is almost as much of a surprise to me as it is to you. I just asked Night as we came down today. Even then it just slipped out."

"You mean you don't want to marry my little girl?"

If looks could kill, Bran was near death. Strange, his Raven didn't appear. This fleeting thought occurred to Bran as he started to explain over again.

"No sir, that's not what I meant. I was talking to her about how she had been so good for me after all my lingering troubles from Vietnam and now I don't know what I'd do if I didn't have her in my life. I love her very much. More than I ever thought could happen to a person."

This much Ferris seemed to know about. "It's the damnedest thing isn't it? How these women can get to you. You think there isn't a one that can bring you to your knees and then along came one with a certain look and wham! You're down for the count."

He chuckled, but immediately his snapping blue eyes turned grim again. In a voice meant to intimidate any jury, he stated, "Again, what are your intentions?"

"I'm an engineer, sir. I bid on, or hire out on any contract that takes my fancy and so far have done a good job on them. I get paid well but I really don't need much money as my folks did investments for me while I was in prison."

"PRISON!"

"Vietcong war prison. I was in there three years before the exchange."

Bran hastily explained before he was cut down by a *Lethal Weapon's* look-alike. Man, where were the flower children: those peace loving people he had heard about? Obviously, it didn't relate to the children of those peace-loving people it they were wronged.

About then, Sunny burst into the room followed closely by her mother.

"Dad! Are you giving Bran a hard time? I've spent all these years trying to find a man I could love. Now you're trying to run him off."

She voiced this with a smile, knowing her father better than Bran did.

"Ah sweetheart! What kind of father would I be if I just rushed you out the door with your young man and said now do it?"

This brought a welcome laugh from everyone.

With a hearty hand shake Ferris gave a friendly smile, "Now Bran, welcome to the family, and I do mean family as many of the old commune people still consider us that, long after the fact. Plus, Mugs brings home troubled people from her line of work. They quickly become possessive of this family and become life-long friends."

There was more general conversation. Then the two young people needed to start for home.

A two-hour drive was ahead of them, and everyone had to work the next day.

Outside, Bran asked Ferris about his MG sports car. "Did you restore your MG, or did you buy it in that mint condition?"

"Restored every last inch of it. Of course it was mine from the beginning, so it was never in bad shape."

The need to leave was not so important as a trip to the garage. Sunny and her mom gave each other the boys-and-their-toys look and went back to the porch swing.

Ferris turned on the lights in the garage. The shop was well equipped. Ferris explained how in the old days, many of the commune people needed something to keep them busy. He had bought everything they needed for repairing anything that needed repairing.

"I even have a foundry out in back in another building. We make parts that need to be made if we can't find them. I've got some guys out there now making custom made parts. It's very expensive but sometimes that's the only way we can get a replacement. It's also the only way some guys can get a start on their new life. My stipulation is that when working here in this garage, they leave enough room for the MG."

They opened the hood of the beautiful sports car. Here gleamed an engine you could really cook a meal on and not use aluminum foil either. Bran appreciated workmanship and told Ferris so.

"Who did the interior? Your tan leather looks new."

"That's another job that can be done here. Mugs has a

complete sewing room upstairs that can be used by anyone wanting to, or needing a job. She had one man needing help. Chuck was a fine upholsterer. She had the sewing room outfitted with everything he needed to get started again. Chuck did the MG for me. We used it to show-off his style until he was able to go out on his own again. That's tanned hide from a little shop in Marysville. We try to keep things local."

"Night didn't tell me about all of this. Just that you both worked to help others and your grandparents stipulated in their wills that the money be used for good causes."

"That's correct. That probably kept Mugs and I on the straight and narrow path when we could have taken all their money and blown it or even given it away. I don't know why we started some of these projects. They just seemed to evolve from need. We were lucky we had the resources to make it all happen. Not much of the equipment is used now but it's still here if anyone needs it."

The two men left the garage, turning off the lights and closing the garage door again.

"Now your 240 Z car looks as good as my MG. I suppose you restored it also, since you were so interest in my car?"

Naturally, they gravitated towards Bran's 'Z' car.

"I restored mine during my recovery from Vietnam. It was the only thing I could do and get so wrapped up in I couldn't think. That and my studies left me little time to remember. It did make me quite a loner as Night probably told you."

Bran opened the door.

"I could use a good upholstery job. Maybe I could get Chuck to do this one for me?"

"Sure, I'll look into it for you."

Ferris and Bran talked about a good color for the 'Z' car's interior. Turquoise to match Night's eyes thought Bran but didn't say it. He didn't know Night's father that well yet.

Running out of time, Bran looked over at the porch swing. There sat the two ladies talking quietly, but looking at the two men as they did. Seeing Bran looked like he was ready to go,

Sunny got up and hugged her mother. She ran down the steps and into her father's arms.

"See you guys soon."

She hugged him and scrabbled into the car.

They entered the Skagit Valley very late in the day. As the sun was sinking in the west, the most beautiful rainbow spanned the valley.

"Look Bran, the rainbow is connecting your heritage with the Ranger Station."

Sure enough, it looked like one end was up where Ross Lake could be and the other might be about where Marblemount Ranger Station was.

"My pot of gold is really you, Night. And we did connect with those two points. Some Irish legends do hold true."

He reached over and laid his hand on her knee squeezing it a little. Not to be outdone, Sunny reached over and kissed him on the cheek.

CHAPTER 17

BRAN'S REPORT

The next day Sunny went out on her next backcountry patrol. While she was gone it rained and was totally miserable weather. Since she and her partner were prepared for this type of weather, it was something they could handle. It just made for a messy cleanup after they got back.

Bran worried about her. This was something new to him. Never had he worried about anyone while on this type of job. Totally alone and totally a loner was what he had been. Could he handle having to worry about someone else again? If the nightmares didn't come back, he was probably all right. It was a good test for him. Never would he want to inflict his nightmares on his Night.

Meanwhile, he prepared his presentation on the cabin he and Night found. He did the work up on the information they had pertaining to the cabin and his long lost relatives. Although, they would never know the true story, he was sure the cabin was Great-grandfather's place of birth. That was enough to know as it belonged to the park now. This would be the best preservation anyone could ask for.

He now had pictures of the cradle. His uncle's family, a cousin wasn't about to give it up even for historical purposes. He didn't blame them. The picture showed it was an incredible piece of craftsmanship even with the chips and dents in it. It had held many babies over the years, plus some dolls and a few cats. His cousin's letter stated it had held plants, were those water stains? And now held a collection of magazines until another first born son came along.

He had copies of the newspaper article he and Night found in Seattle. The one about a couple found drowned in the Skagit River. The man had been wrapped in a bearskin rug. The woman had been tangled in the ropes tied to it. The most notable of all had been the matching wedding bands of hammered gold nuggets. With the diaries corroborating both the rings, the bearskin wrapped around the man and the dated entry of the diary, it was reasonable to presume it was Rafe and Katy Donovan.

The baby in the cradle found by Eli Swift-River must surely be his Great-grandfather Moses. The time of the year and approximate age of the baby tied in. It was strange how his great-grandfather and his great-great uncle had been born about the same time. It was hard to convert 'moons' to days of the month but he knew from the stories, it had been near the end of summer.

Then when the River Spirit's baby appeared, it coincided with the fish run near the end of fall. Again, the diary and the sweat lodge stories coincided. Bran hated to take all this to the head ranger without Night, but he had held off long enough. It was his job and it was part of his investigation.

Jake Simms, the head ranger shook hands with Bran.

"What's the problem, Bran?"

Bran quietly closed the door to the office and leaned some tools up against the desk.

"No problem really just a find I need to tell you about, but

I don't think you'll want the rest of the outfit to know until we figure out how to handle this."

"Okay, tell me about it. I'm all ears."

Bran told the ranger the incredible story. He pulled out all his evidence, including the pictures Night had taken when they first discovered the cabin. From a box, he took out the wedding dress and baby coat that was still wrapped around the Delft pitcher. The few tools leaning against the desk were obviously very old. The wedding picture of the couple found in the diaries brought a gasp from Jake Simms.

"Hell Bran, this looks just like you after a week on the trail. Just whose picture is this?"

On that observation, Bran told the ranger he thought this find really was part of his own heritage. It all seemed incredible to Jake. He was very excited about it all though.

"This would be a great addition to our proposed museum."

He got up and came around the desk.

"You say you can take me there without any trouble?"

"Sure, but I'll need to prepare a ladder to get down into the cave. Even an aluminum ladder would do. In fact an eight foot one would do just fine and be easy to tote too."

Bran was mentally thinking, of all the things they might need as he was talking. Jake was mentally doing some calculations, too.

"I really need to take our park naturalist along. He will be the one to do most of the follow up on your cabin, plus do the planning for what might happen to it in the future."

Jake scratched his head. "However, he's gone for a week to get his kid ready for college in Eastern Washington. I don't want to put this off or I won't be able to go with you. Let's do it now, like tomorrow morning—early."

Jake quickly started putting things away in his closet. He was very careful of the wedding dress, hanging it on one of his hangers, slightly askew, then did the same with the tiny baby coat.

"We'll keep this our little secret for now, as you say, everyone would be up there tomorrow if we let the cat-out-of-the-bag too soon. Now let's go round up what we'll need for tomorrow."

Bran watched the excited fellow. He was saddened a little, as the cabin would no longer be his and Night's. It would belong to the world to view as they saw fit. The two men got their gear together in preparation for an early start the next day.

Watching the Ranger leave, Bran knew Simms would tell his wife as soon as he walked in the door. The excitement would have to be shared or Simms would burst. His wife would keep it quiet until it was time to tell the story to the world. She was one fine woman.

They left early the next morning as planned for the long drive up the canyon and the hike along Ross Lake. Jake was almost as excited at getting out of the office for the day as he was about the reason for the outing.

"Not a very good day for a hike but what the hell—I'm out of that damned office at least," grinned the head Ranger. He drove like a maniac, not fast but gawking at everything, accelerating in weird places and generally making Bran hang on for dear life.

Here he had worried about Night surviving the wet and cold, when she should be worrying about his survival just driving with this madman. He hoped they arrived in one piece. He hoped he lived to see Night one more time. Thank god, the parking lot was right up ahead. If they didn't go over the bank parking, he was safe for now.

The two men hiked well together carrying the ladder between them. It wasn't heavy, just awkward. The rain was soon dripping off their ponchos and into their eyes. It didn't dull Jake's eyes. He was too excited to let anything like a little rain ruin his day. The usual couple of hours took them to the meadow.

Bran instructed, "We'll go up over the cliff. It might be better if we took turns with the ladder because the brush will get in the way as we traverse the hillside."

Bran took the ladder as he said this. It wasn't too long until they were at the top of the cliff. Bran stopped short nearly impaling Jake with the butt of the ladder.

Astounded he said, "My god, will you look at this?"

Jake came up beside Bran. The whole side of the hill had slid into the ravine, complete with stumps, vine maple trees and dirt. One big Douglas Fir lay the length of the slide; it's roots sticking ten feet into the air. The solid, bare rock of the cliff was all that was left where the men stood.

"It's my guess we'll never make it into the cave today," observed Bran as he surveyed the ruins with his eyes, his free hand akimbo his hip.

"Why the hell not?" The head Ranger looked like the little kid who had his candy taken away from him.

Bran explained. "The opening to the cave should be about where the middle of the tree is. I'd guess there is about eight to ten feet of mud under that."

He looked around a little more. "Come on, we can at least go farther down around this mess and assess how things look."

Bran put the ladder down. "Let's leave the packs too. No need to take chances on slipping with these on."

The two men made their way down to the path Night and Bran had used to find the cave. It hadn't been easy.

"This path is really the pipeline used to take water from the falls and put it in a reservoir to be pumped up into the cabin area. Night found this when she looked under an exposed area and discovered piping," explained Bran.

"Who the hell is this Night you keep talking about? Some friend of yours?"

"Oh! Sorry Simms, I keep forgetting she has another name. That's Sunny Day. She's the one I told you about, who found the piece of pottery that started the whole thing."

"You're weird Donovan. I know summer folks get nicknames but usually they're close to the original. If not, they're chosen for some stupid prank they pulled."

Jake might have been the head ranger on this base, but at

that moment glancing at Bran, seeing the scowling withdrawal of the taciturn man, even a head Ranger knew enough to shut up. It was that look that made Custer have his last stand with the Indians.

Ignoring Simms, Bran explained further.

"Our cave entrance was up near the face of the cliff on this side. It will take days to remove enough slide material to get to the cave opening. In fact, it might be easier to remove the rocks down in the meadow in front of the cabin by the face of the cliff, rather than try to remove this unstable material."

"I'll tell you one thing, Bran. You've got rocks in your head if you think this mess will be removed without an act of congress. It would take a lot of man-hours and environmental studies to get this job done. This is the usual 'Act of God'—A-la-natural, and all that type of regulation's crap. History comes second to nature in this case." Jake's disappointed tirade ended with a woe-be-gone slump to his shoulders.

In his heart, Bran was relieved. Not only was the cabin to be spared the invasion of people but; he didn't see his Raven in this time of stress. Things were improving for him at least.

Jake headed back up the hill. "No use getting our butts any wetter that they are. Let's head for home and a hot shower."

Bran followed, then picked up the ladder at the top. The way Simms was moving, he would probably have to drag the ladder all the way to the truck by himself. And now! Just what was he going to tell Night? Was he disappointed or ecstatically happy?

CHAPTER *18*

ROMANTIC DREAMS

This week had been a long one for Sunny. The rain beat down on the two girls, with only short breaks from the overcast skies. Holed up in the small backpack tent each night was claustrophobic. Cooking on the small gas stove, with just her head sticking out, was awkward. The only good thing that came of it was her ability to think and dream about Bran.

Her dreams were very graphic, drawn on her eyelids in Technicolor. She had read enough romance books to do justice to these images. How much longer would it be before experiencing these delights in real life? The thought both frightened her and thrilled her. At her age, she should know what love was all about. But love of the heart was something she didn't know about: only friendship love.

They had met a few brave hikers on the Thunder Creek trail. The trail wasn't bad, just long. Being down under the trees for over five miles was depressing in the rain. After that, the climb up hill seemed easier just being out in the open.

They had visited the Rock Cabin on Fisher Creek built by another old timer. This cabin was on the trail, so visited a lot. While they cleaned the area, removing some graffiti, Sunny was reminded of the cabin she and Bran had discovered.

When it was given to the world, would it have graffiti and litter dumped around it? What a shame! Sunny wished there were some way to preserve it but, also, allow the public to see authentic pioneer ways. The Thunder Creek Trail intersected the Cascade Crest Trail. The rest of the way to Rainy Pass was uneventful. At Rainy Pass the sun came out, making the view of white capped mountains spectacular. They spent the day drying out their tents and wet clothing, while working the area.

The Crummy met them on time making everyone happy. Not always was the transportation reliable. So many emergencies cropped up which could affect timing. Radio contact at all times was a big help. The days of the old hand crank telephone must have been a real trial, and sometimes by fire, estimating how many fires must have gone through these areas in the past hundred years. Telephone lines could still be seen in some remote areas. It was part of their job to remove the lines if any were found.

Arriving back at the Ranger Station, they headed for the showers. Thank heavens they were on staggered shifts. If all the crews came in at the same time, there would be nothing but cold water for the last person. Sunny made sure she wasn't the last person. There was a certain big lug she wanted to see as soon as possible.

By now, most of the crew knew she and Bran were friends. How could they help but know, when Sunny's eyes lit up whenever she mentioned him. She still hadn't told anyone about being engaged or about the cave, only where they had researched.

With her hair still wet from her shower, she hurried out the back door of the crew quarters. There sat Bran in one of his lawn chairs drinking out of an enclosed cup. Having an audience made the two of them circumspect.

"Hi there, Night. Come on over, I've got a steak waiting for someone who needs a good meal."

He reached out a hand to guide her to a chair. She welcomed the comfort.

"Man, I hope you mean me big guy. I could eat a horse but I hope it's a large rare beef steak."

"You're in luck. All the horses are too healthy to eat. We're having dead cow. I'm sure that makes you feel better."

Bran turned to the grill that was waiting for the steaks to be slapped on.

"Yuck! I guess I asked for that one. And Bran, you just made a joke. Keep that up and everyone will begin to think you're an all right guy."

Sunny laughed: a tinkling sound that mimicked a small, mountain-brook.

Putting the steaks on the grill, Bran sat down beside Sunny. His hand slid down her arm to squeeze her hand before letting go. The two gazed into each other's eyes. It wasn't easy to make love with your eyes in front of others, who might be watching. The two did it and hoped others were too busy fixing their own supper to pay much attention.

Almost whispering, Bran said, "God I missed you."

"I know, Bran. I thought about you every night, and those thoughts were really special."

Sunny's could feel her cheeks burn.

"I can't believe it, you're blushing. Man, what kind of thoughts were you having about me?"

Bran had no idea he was saying something to Sunny that might embarrass her. Sunny jumped out of her chair to playfully pound on his arm. Grabbing her arm, he pulled her down onto his lap.

"Whoa little girl. I didn't mean to embarrass you. I'm teasing you because I've had such delicious dreams about you, also"

It was nice being in Bran's lap but knowing she couldn't stay there, she got up and sat down in the chair that had been given her. She held the knowledge of the special little hug he gave her to herself.

The one crewmember watching quipped at this interchange.

"Hey Bran, watch it. She's little but mighty. She must get her practice from keeping those kindergartners of hers in line. She has most of us keeping our hands to ourselves, too."

He then went in the crew-house with his own steak to eat.

Bran got up and turned their steaks. A few seconds later, he forked them onto the plates.

"Come on, let's go inside to eat. I've got some more news to tell you."

Inside, he had the table set in the small booth. He took a salad out of the refrigerator, then poured her a glass of her favorite white wine, into a real wineglass.

"I can microwave a baked potato if you would like?"

"Oh no Bran. This looks so good, especially since I've had nothing fresh for a week. It was sweet of you to think of me coming in tired and hungry."

Sweet of him! Hah! All he could think of was getting her alone all week. If she only knew all his thoughts, she would more than hit him on the arm, she would probably skin him alive, then make him run naked and skinless down the road and out of her sight.

"It wasn't sweet of me, Night. It was one way to get you over here to tell you all that has happened this last week without the whole crew knowing."

Too hungry to wait, Sunny started to cut up her streak. News wasn't half as exciting as a good steak. With the bite in her mouth, she mumbled through the juices.

"What's this news you have for me?"

Calmly swallowing his bite before talking, he happened to glance up at Night. Her two hands held both the fork and knife at ridged alert on the table. Her eyes were flashing laser blue sparks. If he didn't tell her quickly, he would be the next bite she took and a piece of his anatomy would be missing for sure.

"Okay, okay! Simms, you know the head Ranger, and I went up to the cave. Guess what?"

A nod from Sunny, "AND?"

"And there had been a slide that covered the cave entrance. It was a bad one. Simms felt there would have to be an Act of Congress to get it dug out."

"Wow! That's something. Now what will happen?"

"Well, Simms said he would just send in a report about it. We'll file all the information with the Park Naturalist. They will tag the evidence. I've taken copies of everything we did and more pictures of the things we brought out. Simms didn't think I could claim any of those things, as there is no real proof that it was Great-grandfather's. It really is enough to know in our minds what happened. Plus, it will be preserved for now even if it isn't the way we thought it might be."

He took another bite of his steak and a sip of the white wine.

"The crew will only know what we found, not where it was found. That way there won't be any rumors of where it's at so ruin-hunters won't get in there and try to dig it out when no one is looking."

"I think that's great. Like your mines, if it's ever needed, it's there for the people in the future. We brought out enough for a display in a museum if one ever gets started. It will be like the '*Lost Dutchman Mine*'; something that is there but its whereabouts is a mystery. Everyone loves a mystery."

Sunny's eyes took on a dreamy look. She could still see the cabin with Bran on the bed waiting for her. Meanwhile, Bran's imagination had his Night in the old-fashioned tub with the water they had heated, taking that nude bath like Bran had. He would have gotten a double threat for her shadow would have been projected against the wall by the lantern light. Slowly dripping water down her slender body—Ahhhhh!

"Do you want to go to bed," said Bran with pain in his voice?

"What?"

Sunny's eyes became focused again.

"That was sure romantic. DO YOU WANT TO GO TO BED? Just like that. Oh sure, I want to go to bed but, in my own bed.

When you can think of a little romance to go with that statement, call me again. I may love you, you big dolt, but I need a little more than DO YOU WANT TO GO TO BED."

Sunny knew she was babbling again, but she was nervous and angry. *Go to bed,* were wild words she didn't know how to handle. She got up and slammed out the door, completely forgetting Bran was left with the dirty dishes yet to do.

Bran just sat there. What in holy hell did he think he was doing? He had just blabbed out the most ridiculous invitation. This was the woman he loved with all of his new and tender heart. She had reacted predictably to the foolish invitation.

He found her over by the volleyball game. She hadn't joined in since it was nearly quitting time due to darkness. She watched him come over, but turned her head back towards the game.

"I'm sorry Night. That, was the most asinine thing I've ever said: I was imagining being up at the cabin with the lamp light on you, when I went off the deep end and just blurted out my thoughts. I love you too much for such a solicitous suggestion. Forgive me?"

"Bran, I'm sorry too. I was just frustrated. I had thoughts of you up at the cabin: on the bed—and then you made that suggestion. I didn't know what to do—so I ran. We both have a lot to learn about this romance stuff. It's new to me and you're just learning again. Let's go back to the lawn chairs and finish our talk."

Bran took Sunny's arm. She leaned against him slightly as they walked back to the chairs. They sat down, the warm night wrapping around them.

"Next weekend is Great-grandfather's one hundredth birthday party. It's also, the ceremony of the return of the summer-run Chinook salmon. Try to free up your weekend, or trade days off. Be sure to invite your parents, as that will be when all the big announcements are made. With your permission, I would like to announce our engagement. I know we've hardly had any romance, as you put it, but I don't want to lose you now that I've found you."

Again, Bran reached over and squeezed her hand. It was tough not to breach the edicts dictated by the jobs they were in.

"I would love that, Bran. I'll call my folks as soon as I go in. They will come and I won't even have to tell them about the announcement. They will come for your Great-grandfather's big day."

She reached her foot over and rubbed it against his. There were so many erotic things to do when they seemed to be forbidden. A glance of the eye, a touch, a bump and even rubbing her shoe against his seemed sexy. She could hardly wait for the hot-and-heavy stuff, whatever that was.

CHAPTER 19

CENTENNIAL

A beautiful day heralded the birthday party. Bran stepped from his motor home. His eyes swept the wide valley. The old B and W burn on Lookout Mountain hardly showed anymore. He had been told it had been an eyesore for twenty years. Two men had died on that fire. A testimony for the people of Marblemount just how devastating a forest fire could be, and this one was deliberately caused my man himself.

Across the Cascade River was located the fish hatchery. Like young sailors waiting, the tiny fish practiced their jumping before being let loose to go to sea. There to become the mighty salmon we all enjoy eating in the Pacific Northwest. The huge Chinook salmon was starting to show up in the river now. Some of these salmon would be cooked for the Centennial birthday party later today.

Cow heaven was behind the Ranger Station. It was said, local farmers ran their herds of cattle up there during the summers in past years. Another story had these same farmers, taking some of the herds up the Skagit River to summer feed them on Jack Mountain in the Ross Lake area. That was over fifty miles just to get to the lake. Now that was a feat that seemed impossible, but local people even remembered them doing it. Pioneers were strong people. Bran contemplated all this while breathing in the fresh air, with the smell of autumn in it. It was strange how you could just step outside one day and smell fall in the air. You didn't have to be part Indian to know this either. That's right! He wasn't part Indian anymore. He felt like Great-grandfather; you didn't stop being what you were raised as, just because someone or something said that you weren't. Now, wasn't that a complicated thought?

Everything was ready. His parents had come in from Colorado and were down at the Homestead. Night's parents would be up from Everett for the party. He would pick Night up and take her down with him about ten o'clock this morning.

He proceeded to jog down the road. He needed the exercise. This last week had been nothing but paper work. His job was nearly done here. He had another one lined up back on the East Coast, about finding an old jail site. He happened to see the advertisement in the paper just the other day. He didn't need this new job, but it sounded like fun. Would Night think it was fun? Man-o-man! Would he never learn? He had forgotten to discuss this new part of his life with her.

He was getting winded so slowed down to a fast walk. He laughed to himself. He was learning. If he surprised her with something she didn't know about, he could expect retaliation. It would pay him to learn to be honest and open with her.

Sunny spent the morning mooning over what to wear. Her first time to meet Bran's parents and what did she have to wear? Nothing! She decided to wear the turquoise gauze dress again. At least it was comfortable, and Bran said it matched her eyes.

Just a few more days of work and her job would be over. *No Fraternizing, Among the Help*, would be over too. She planned to take that handsome Bran down and really show him how she felt about him. She might not know much about love but Boy-O-Boy would she learn fast.

Tingles, she never knew about, sailed through her body. If this was the beginning of love, she could hardly wait to feel the rest of it.

Ten o'clock came and the two met in the driveway by the 'Z' car. They couldn't help the quick hug they gave each other. One of the office personnel just happened to be looking out the window. She smiled at the couple's antics but didn't call it to anyone's attention. To see love blossoming was a universal lift to anyone's spirits. The young couple had just made her day brighter.

Bran and Sunny enjoyed the drive down to the party. They drove past the little park where they had talked. Past the turnoff to Rockport, a historic place on the river, and on to Concrete known for its hay-days of the cement plants that built the dams and others in the state too. Hamilton and Lyman were old logging settlements. Sedro Woolley was a double saw mill town until it was combined making it into one small city. The day was beautiful. The two people enjoyed their ride together and the peace and quiet of this short time together.

The celebration for Bran's Great-grandfather's birthday, coincided with the celebration of the return of the salmon. This year it was being held near the ocean at the delta of the Skagit River.

The elders of the tribe started the ceremony with talks and dances. It made more sense to the tribe members, than to the watching bystanders. However, the launching of the canoe, with Moses Swift riding in it was a sight to behold. Obviously, a very elderly man, revered by the way he was handed into the canoe, commanded the respect of all. He was splendid in his robe and eagle feathered headdress.

The canoe was paddled into the middle of what was probably the river. The skeletal remains of the first salmon caught this year, was held high over Moses' head. Some chanting could be heard. Then with great and ancient ceremony, it was lowered into the river, tail first towards the ocean, head pointed toward the Skagit River. It was said, this way the salmon knew which way to return to the mighty river.

Bran's Great-grandfather had rallied forth to do this honor one more time. At the story telling, he had related the tale told to him. How through the ages there had been this baby of the River Spirit. It had been given into the care of the tribe. As long as that baby was alive and well cared for, the mighty salmon would always return to the Skagit. He had always known that he was that baby: after all, the great salmon was in his care.

He then explained in a voice quickly losing its power, how his great-grandson had discovered his true heritage by revelations of the Raven. Much murmuring could be heard. When he raised the picture of his biological parents, a gasp could be heard. Many people turned to look at Bran. It wasn't hard to imagine Bran with a beard.

Moses explained, he no longer thought his powers could help the tribe as his blood was no longer Indian, only in his heart did he belong to the tribe. It was time to pass his gift to another worthy person.

Sunny, listening to all the stories told could well understand how you could fall under the spell of folklore. Her parents could feel it too. They had their arms around their daughter as if to protect her from a legend that might pack her off. During Bran's turn on the podium, she understood more fully what a specter his Raven had been.

At the end of his legend, he told them what a help Sunny Day had been. Here he stuttered a little still thinking of her as 'Night'.

He then announced, "I'd like you all to know that having found this lovely lady, I'm hoping she will consent to be my bride. She is my soul mate."

It seemed to be more of a destiny to Sunny in this environment to hear this announcement. She was called to the podium by Bran to be shown off. It was worth it by the big hug she received from him when she got there. Everyone applauded this event. There were tears of joy in the eyes of both sets of parents.

Following the ceremonies was the feast. Venison and elk meat was on spits being roasted. Salomon, clams, oysters and crab were on the menu, plus, many inventive side dishes. It was all you could eat and delicious.

Bran's parents were the kind anyone could love. His dad's boisterous laughter could be heard over the lapping of the waves. His mother, though quiet, had a warm heart and was courteous and kind to everyone. She told Sunny, she would forever be grateful to her for bringing Bran out of his shell.

"I only hope he doesn't come out of his shell as far as his noisy father. Two of them would be too much."

She said this with a loving smile as the booming laughter could be heard again. Sunny laughed over this observation.

Sunny's parents fitted right in with this group. They had always been outgoing people. It wasn't long before Ferris found someone to talk tribal law with. Margarete or Mugs as she preferred to be called, found other do-gooders to trade stories and solutions with.

Bran's sister was like her dad and could tell one joke after another. Her jokes sometimes lost the punch line as she ran over to settle a dispute between her children, or even someone else's child. She was tall and dark like Bran and her mother. Her children were a mixed bag with one urchin having bright red hair and further signs of being like his Irish grandfather.

Would she have children like that or would they look like Bran? Sunny mused over this as she watched all the things going on around her. She felt arms come around her in a bone crushing hug.

"Night love, I need a kiss. I've watched your lovely face long enough."

Bran was kissing her neck as he spoke. He turned her round and proceeded to kiss her more lover-like.

"Why do you do this to me when so many people are around," she whispered.

"I want to take you down and kiss you all over your body, rip your clothes off and have my wicked way with you."

Bran groaned. "You are a wicked woman saying those things to me. All I dream about anymore is the two of us doing just that and you stand there and tell me that in broad daylight with hundreds of people around."

Sunny giggled. "Fun isn't it? Teasing you is getting to be my fantasy. Can you imagine—the first of the summer, I thought you hated me for teasing you and now I'm still teasing you and you love it."

She leaned back in his arms and slowly licked her lips while looking into his eyes.

"You minx. I still don't know why I noticed you then. Others might have tried to flirt with me and I wouldn't have paid any attention. It just happened to be you I noticed and my ire just flipped. Sometimes now, I don't even recall that I was anything but a deliriously happy person."

The party was breaking up. Little kids were getting fretful. All in all, it had been a wonderful one hundred-year celebration. Old Moses, having been excused from the rest home for a few days, was going back to the Homestead under the watchful eye of his family.

Bran's sister wasn't the airhead she projected and had video taped most of the ceremony. While she had contact with Old Moses, she was going to encourage him to tell more tales of both his life and any folklore he knew. She was starting to be the family historian and genealogist. Her astute questioning could get your life story in two minutes flat.

All hoped Moses wouldn't have a relapse but with a nurse for a granddaughter, no one was going to worry about it. She kept him resting whenever possible.

Sunny and Bran drove back up the Skagit to Marblemount Ranger Station, recapping the day's events and laughing a lot. Bran pulled over to the rest stop just outside Marblemount. He just had to cuddle Night some more.

"Come here you lovely woman."

He ran his fingers sensually down her cheek. It was like satin. She smelled of flowers. Their kiss was long and hard, changing to softness as it went on. Bran's one hand was slowly making its way under her skirt. It had just made it to the juncture of her femininity, when Sunny jumped back.

"Bran. I'm not sure what happens next. Or even if anything should happen next."

"You're right Night. This isn't the time or place to let this get too far. My old hand just has a mind of its own. Sorry love."

"That's okay Bran." Thinking of a distraction, "See that church up there. That's where I would like to get married when the time comes."

Seeing the picturesque setting, Bran could see why she liked it.

"I think that's a wonderful idea. It looks like a place you and I would pick to be married in; small, cozy and in the mountains. Let's go home and think about it."

CHAPTER 20

MARBLEMOUNT DANCE

Labor Day weekend had the scheduled annual dance at Marblemount Community Hall. Sunny was supposed to have gone home. Her duties were over. She had stayed the extra days just to go to the dance with Bran. He told her they were fun even if he hadn't danced at them. To visit with the people had made him feel more human this last year.

This time she was told she could wear her blue jeans or anything she wanted. The dance was very informal. Bring something for the potluck table was the rule. Of course you didn't have to, but that was what made it so social. She had found all this out by talking to the ladies of the Ranger Station.

Children weren't invited to this party, as it was a BYOB. The ladies said baby sitters were found so they could have a night out for a change. Many of the husbands would still be on call, but could come since it was in town, not more than a mile away from the station, assessable by both radio and telephone.

Sunny and Bran arrived at the community center about

nine thirty that evening. The band had just started playing. Sunny put her deviled eggs on the food table with the rest of the snacks. Bran deposited the bachelor's standard bag of chips on the table. Sunny snickered to herself. At a bachelor party there probably wasn't anything but chips and beer.

The many tables, placed around the room, were full but with some shuffling, space was made available for them. The band was good. Soon Sunny's feet were tapping to the rhythm. To her surprise, Bran asked her to dance right away. He was a good dancer, although slightly stiff to start with.

"Where did you learn to dance so well?" Sunny asked.

"I wasn't always the stoic man you thought I was. I led a wild life in the first college years. Life was fun and so was I. It's just hard to remember that after all this time has elapsed."

He did a quick turn swinging her raven hair out in wings. She caught her breath and then smiled.

"Well I'm glad old Methuselah isn't too old to dance anymore. I love to dance. The commune people danced all the time. Someone always had a fiddle or guitar to strum"

They danced many of the dances until break time for the band. During this time, people who played instruments, sometimes went up and kept the music going until the band came back after their break. Unbeknownst to Sunny, this happened many times during the winter months. She was just about to find this fact out.

One fellow from the Ranger Station went up to discuss something with the band. Next thing Sunny knew, there was a call for Bran to come up to the podium. Bran reluctantly went up. Soon, Bran was playing the electric guitar.

His music was more to sing by. And sing Bran did in his baritone voice that made Sunny shiver. Soon people were both dancing and singing away. It didn't matter that the singers were out of tune or a dancer was out of step, or even that a few old timers were dancing on their own. Everyone was having a good time.

It seemed to be time to eat, also. The ladies put more food on the table. Coffee could be smelled freshly brewed. People lined up, filling their plates, then finding a seat again. Diehard dancers couldn't be bothered to eat. Sunny fixed a plate, since her partner was busy playing the guitar. Soon the band came back and Bran was freed from his acquired duty. He received handshakes and back slaps before he made it back to the table. Sunny kissed his cheek.

"You were wonderful Bran. I didn't know you would sing in front of people."

"It's strange. I might not have been able to talk to anyone, but when asked, it never bothered me to sing. I didn't always take requests because that would be interacting with someone, and I couldn't take that pressure. I just sang whatever I was in the mood for. Did you happen to notice that most of those songs tonight were love songs?"

"No I didn't. I thought you always sang this type of song. That's what you sang to me in the car that time."

Both took a minute to remember. It had been one of the times love had entered into their relationship. Bran leaned over and rubbed his nose against hers.

"I remember very well, Night and I'm remembering again what we were doing. Let's go home." He whispered in her ear.

Sunny took her egg plate and left with Bran. It was getting late so no one cared, except for a couple of good nights called after them.

They got in the car and drove back to the Ranger Station. Bran parked in his usual place.

"Do you want to come in? I don't have to work tomorrow and you're leaving for home after this weekend. We need to talk about our future."

"Sure Bran. Let's go in and talk."

In the motor home all thought of talk went by the wayside. Bran took Sunny in his arms. He was kissing her as he kept stepping back towards the bedroom. The light didn't even get turned on. The only light came from the outside building, showing through the curtained windows. Sunny's legs hit the end of the bed.

"Whoops!"

The two fell down on it bouncing around a little but not caring in the least. Bran started to remove Sunny's shirt while she fumbled around for his buttons. Luckily his western shirt snapped, and popped open with a quick pull.

They got each other's shirts off breathing hard all the time. Bran ran his hands through her long hair. It felt so silky. What would that feel like sliding around over his body? No thought of his scars came to him. He was so wrapped up in loving his Night.

"Bran, there is something I should tell you before we go any further."

"And what's that love?" Bran breathed into her hair. His eyes were glazed as feelings washed over him.

"I'm a virgin, Bran. I don't know much about what comes next."

"A virgin? How could you reach this age and still be a virgin?" Bran was hoping he hadn't heard her correctly.

"Well, in the commune I was protected by more family than I care to think about. All of them preached safe sex and love your partner. I didn't find anyone to love so I didn't have to practice safe sex either."

Oh god, he hadn't thought about safe sex. He hadn't thought about anything. Sunny sat up on the bed crossing her legs, yoga fashion. Bran couldn't sit up yet. He lay on his back with his hands over his eyes. His voice was slightly scratchy sounding.

"A virgin. Night love, if you think I'm going to ruin the most wonderful gift a woman can give to her man, you've got to be crazy. That gift should be saved for the man you love and that man should be your husband."

He moved his arm enough to peek out from under it at her lovely face.

"But you're going to be my husband. I'm just inexperienced, not stupid."

Sunny's voice was quivering slightly by now.

Bran rolled over onto his stomach, crossed his arms, tipped his head back and looked up at her.

"Shhh, darling girl I know I'm going to be your husband, I want to be your husband, but I'm not your husband yet. I also, am not going to defile a girl who's, dad looks like Mel Gibson. His *Lethal Weapon* retaliation might be more that we both want."

His voice came out in a frustrated cry. He jumped up and started pacing down the hall, into the living room, flinging his arms up in the air in a sign of being thwarted.

Well, so much for his manhood coming out of hibernation, thought Bran. He would probably shrink up to the point he'd be peeing like a woman, cringing at his very crude thoughts.

He was finally brought to his knees by a slip of a woman, when the whole Vietcong army hadn't been able to do it.

Bran came back and sat on the end of the bed. A contrite Sunny, watched Bran sitting holding his head.

"I'm sorry about being a virgin. I didn't know it would be such a big deal to you."

She grabbed his hands in hers. "I'm sorry Bran."

"Sorry! Sorry about being a virgin! My god, Night, that's the most wonderful thing a man could want. I'll gladly wait for my present until we're married. It isn't easy, when the woman you want sits there on your bed looking so beautiful, with her face flushed by love and her hair mussed from my fingers running through it. Just looking at you turns me on."

Smiling at him, she said, "Honestly Bran, I wouldn't mind you coming back to bed to make love to me."

"No love. I respect you and your parents, plus your extended family for teaching you the value of love over sex. I guess my gift to you will be my frustrated waiting until we can get married." To himself, he thought, and when I can get a truckload of condoms.

He cracked a lop-sided smile that melted Sunny to a puddle. Then it turned slightly wicked.

"How about tomorrow? We could hop in the car and drive all day to Idaho or how about right now and drive all night?"

The tension was broken by his teasing remarks.

"No big fellow. My mother would be more a threat to you with that idea than my Mel Gibson look-alike father. If you think you can beat her out of a big party, think again. We would have to leave the country with that Bantam hen on our tail. It's all she's talked about since we told her our news. If we don't hurry up and decide: when is a good time to get married, she will have a guest list longer than it already is."

Sunny threw her arms wide to show the extent of the list.

"The whole commune has been told about their little Sunny getting married. Even if it's a the life-style they haven't chosen, they're happy for me and need to give me luv-hugs. Now come here and lay your head on my lap."

Grabbing the end of the quilt spread, Bran rolled over bringing it around him and his love. His head came down on her lap. A contented sigh escaped from his lips as Sunny ran her fingers over his forehead and into his soft dark hair. It wasn't long until she slipped down cuddling Bran's head with her whole body as they slept.

CHAPTER 21

THE WEDDING

Sunny went back to Everett to her teaching job. She would work until December, at which time she could break her contract. She wanted to be with Bran after they were married. She could substitute teach wherever he needed to go. During their long talks, they decided they could even do Peace Corp work if they wanted to. Her folks would let them park the motor home on their property. There were several places already set up for mobile unites, again due to the commune years.

Meanwhile, Bran did all the work to wind down his project. He would finish by December. In conjunction with the Historical Society, the town back East, said that spring would be a good time to find their jail site and maybe have a few more small projects like that for him.

The Historical Society had been thrilled to get him at the small price he negotiated with them. He was getting excited about his next project, as he would have Night with him. He would always think of her as 'Night' and the many nights coming to them in the future would only reinforce that sensual name to him.

Sunny and Bran were married in October at the Episcopal Church near Rockport. This was the little white church Sunny had first seen at the rest stop that early day in June, so many months ago. It had taken awhile to find a minister to marry them there, since neither were Episcopalians. Her mother came to the rescue with her many connections. The board of trustees of the church voted to allow them to use the facilities for the nondenominational church wedding.

As the church was small, only close friends and relatives, plus a few from the Ranger Station were invited. Even then, the church bulged to overflowing. There would be more parties sponsored by individuals, such as Sunny's parents with the whole ex-commune and Bran's parents with his side of the family. Even the Ranger Station ladies had given Sunny and Bran a shower prior to the wedding.

As they made their promises to each other, they were framed in the picturesque half-moon memorial window of the church. While in the back ground, the majestic Eldorado Mountain could be seen as the sentinel overlooking the valley. The knotty pine paneling and wooden pews added to the old fashioned wedding.

If you happened to be looking out of the window and not at the two people being married, you would have seen two ravens circling the valley, seeing all, knowing all.

Sunny looked lovely in the old fashioned cream colored wedding dress of Bran's Great-great-grandmother Katy's. A skillful seamstress had been found to take the dress in and hem it, but allow all the seams to be taken out later to let the dress reshape itself back to normal. After all, it was still the property of the National Park Service. Everyone thought it wouldn't hurt it to be used one more time by the people responsible for finding it in the first place.

Her attendants were dressed in a lovely shade of turquoise. All held branches of the vine maple with their blazing autumn colors and a few purple mums skillfully woven into the bouquets.

Sunny's bouquet held baby's breath, just a few autumn leaves with purple mums cascading down the cream colored streamers. Her hat had been found in an antique store her mother frequented. It was old fashioned with a wide brim, netting around the crown, one side rolled up slightly making room for the bower of flowers it held.

Her something new was an amethyst and turquoise necklace, given to her by Bran's parents. After seeing the lovely necklace given to Sunny, for something borrowed, her mother had loaned her the family amethyst ring for her right hand.

Bran had grown a beard just for the wedding. He could hardly wait to shave it off. With the beard and the slightly old fashioned suit he had rented; he looked much as Rafe had done so many years before. Sunny had wanted their wedding picture to resemble the ancient one found in the Bible. She almost had an obsession about this and though he had protested, Bran was pleased. There would be more pictures taken with all their attendants, which would identify the wedding as their own.

Their rings were a surprise for Sunny. Bran had found a goldsmith to make two wedding rings in the shape of a raven with its wings wrapping around the finger. On Sunny's ring the talons were extended to wrap around the diamond in the engagement ring. This was opposite of the way traditional wedding rings were worn, but it fitted so well Bran liked the idea. Sunny was delighted

When they kissed after the ceremony, Bran whispered in her ear.

"You are the most beautiful thing I've ever seen and I love you with all my heart."

"Oh Bran, you are my life and I didn't even know you were out there waiting for me."

"May I introduce you all to the groom and his lovely wife, Mr. and Mrs. Bran Donovan," the minister raised his arms to embrace the congregation.

Clapping started, so the couple broke apart and bowed

slightly to their guests, before proceeding down the aisle with the strains of the organ wheezing its ancient message to all.

They formed a receiving line outside under the towering large leaf maples with their leaves a bright fall yellow. The reception followed in the basement. Sunny's mother had spared no expense for her only daughter. However, she hadn't counted on the local people and Bran's side of the family to bring offerings as they were used to doing. Now the menu and tables were filled to over-flowing and the people were rubbing their full stomachs.

The couple didn't sneak off but left the church among the hail of rice, birdseed and popcorn. Sunny's mother believed in the environment but didn't want to take a chance, so rice was included hoping the offering would mean many grandchildren for her to fuss over. Bran's father grabbed rice for the same reason. He wanted Bran to experience the love of a child as he had done.

As the two left the church in their car decorated with streamers, and a *'Just Married'* sign gracing the back window, two ravens sitting in the top of the huge maple tree, cawed their raucous greeting. Sunny and Bran heard this through their open window. They looked at each other. A joyful laugh issued forth from the happy couple. They waved good-by out the window of the car, both to the by-standers and the two ravens. A whirl of dust followed the two as they went to wherever newly married couples go, while two ravens circled the sky and left the valley to go wherever ravens go.

LOST HERITAGE

A HERITAGE WAS LOST IN THE MOUNTAINS ONE DAY
AND ONLY THE RAVEN KNOWS!
IS GOD THE RAVEN OR IS THE RAVEN GOD?
MAYBE ONLY THE RAVEN KNOWS!
A HUNDRED YEARS LASPED THE NAME FORETOLD
BUT ONLY THE RAVEN KNOWS!
THE BLACK HAIRED MAN MARRIED THE BONNY LASS
AND LAID ALL THE GHOSTS TO REST,
AND THEN THE RAVEN FLEW!

By Robin Wood

EPILOGUE

BACK HOME

Sunny sat in a chair by the window over looking their acreage. She had read in the diaries that Katy Donovan had much the same thing so many years ago. The day was so beautiful and she felt quite well. Her diary was perched on top of her protruding stomach. Everyday she wrote in it. The day she and Bran were married, a compelling force, so strong, made her start writing. Any piece of paper would do, until she finally purchased her first true diary.

She had trouble believing in Bran's Raven but she could almost believe in the Spirit of Katy Donovan. Now she was glad she had started them. Referring back to her diaries sometimes made her point in an argument with Bran. Although, he still laughed and teased her there was a strong attitude about something he deemed right.

Musing back in time, she remembered their first home; a little Cape Cod type house with water crashing against the rocks. Bran had found the jail site for the Historical Society, plus when word got out, he was inundated with small projects like that.

It was kind of a honeymoon time in their life. Sunny had stayed home. Within months she was pregnant with Rafe. Rafe turned out to be a throw-back to Bran's red headed father, an Irish imp, if there ever was one. Their honeymoon was over.

In times of crisis, Bran still had his Raven. At he crucial moment of Rafe's birth, Bran yelled out, "The Raven! The Raven!" The doctors made him sit down and put his head between his legs until Rafe made his first squall. A sheepish, Bran was still the first one to hold the tiny baby.

Sunny applied for a teaching stint in Australia. There Bran was happiest working with the Aborigines. He mapped many trails in conjunction with the historical preservation movement. Sunny loved teaching in the small outback town and managed to get an extension to stay longer. Katy was born there giving her dual citizenship.

Now they were home again. Home to the ten acres her dad had given them when they were first married. Bran's old motor home had been housed in a heated garage all those years and was still in excellent condition.

Bran and Ferris had spent eighteen months building this beautiful log home with its wrap-around, front porch. Sunny looked around the room. The logs were a mellow-yellow, and polished to a sheen. All their pictures and artifacts seemed to blend well with it, from seafaring scenes to Australian art. Just recently at the seaport town of LaConner, they had purchased a picture of a rainbow spanning the Skagit Valley with the mountains in the background. It seemed as though artists though it was a beautiful scene too, just as Sunny and Bran had so many years ago.

One sad note in Sunny's diary was the death of Bran's Great-grandfather Moses. His funeral was an event much like the Centennial birthday party. Sunny, much amazed at the service, recorded every little detail for history. Her children could read about it years from now when they became interested in their heritage.

Her stomach rolled around making writing difficult. Sunny laughed.

"Hey, little guys, you're disturbing my writing."

Big brother, Rafe and sister, Katy, were so thrilled to be getting some new babies. One apiece, they kept saying. Katy was showing signs of being a chip off Sunny's old block. Her daddy absolutely spoiled her rotten.

Bran's comment was, "But she's so much like you, I can't help it."

And Rafe was getting to be more like his grandfather Donovan and could tell 'Knock, knock' jokes until everyone called time-out. His hair still was a blaze of red.

Sunny got up slowly and gazed down at the cradle: the famous cradle. Bran's relatives, when learning of the impending birth of twins, turned over the cradle to Bran. Now she and Bran reminisced every time they looked at it.

Their joke was what to name the twins. If they were girls the names might be harder to find, but of course if they were boys, they would be named Noah and Moses. Even historical names were hard to take sometimes. Then they'd kid around and say, "Well, nicknames are great. NO and MO—no mo' babies at this house," and they would laugh together.

Just then she saw Bran coming across the field. There was a charging animal going straight at him. In Katy's diary this probably would have been the charging bear, a frightening time for her, sighed Sunny. However, Bran welcomed the charge as a huge Black Labrador dog jumped around glad to see him. Sunny smiled, watching Bran cuff the animal's ears and throw a stick to be retrieved. They had called the dog *'Bear'* even if it was named after a tragic historical event. Their cat was called *'Old Molly'* for the mule and was just about as stubborn. They had changed history to a joyful time of life.

THE END—THERE AIN'T NO MO

BVG